SECRETS OF THE PAST

A Pauline Gray Novella

by Louise Bates

FIRST EDITION
ISBN-13: 979-8-9858009-0-6

Cover design by Louise Bates

StarDance Press
stardancepress.com

SECRETS OF THE PAST

CHAPTER ONE

Old Memories and New Friendships

Pauline Gray gathered together the untidy stack of papers on the kitchen table and smiled at the white-haired woman sitting across from her.

"I think we've done a good bit of work today, Miss Lewis."

Anita Lewis's wrinkled cheeks were flushed a pale pink, as they usually were when she and Pauline finished a writing session. Remembering her past brought back a piece of her youth to the elderly woman. "Indeed yes, Miss Gray. I'm ever so grateful to you for taking the time to come help me. It's been such a pleasure talking to you."

"The pleasure has been mine," Pauline told her sincerely.

When Miss Lewis, a former teacher for both grammar and high school, had asked Pauline to help her write the story of her life, Pauline had agreed from practical purposes more than anything else. Miss Lewis was willing to pay, and Pauline couldn't turn down the chance to fill out her slim purse. In the year 1934, few people could.

As the days and weeks passed, the twice-a-week sessions of Miss Lewis reminiscing and Pauline taking notes shorthand to be typed into a coherent narrative later had become more than a job. Pauline grew deeply interested in the tale of this woman's life, from her idyllic childhood on the family's dairy farm, to a difficult girlhood trying to raise her younger siblings after her mother passed away when she was fifteen, to the winning of her independence with a scholarship to Elmira College, to the romance cut short when her fiancé died in a tragic accident on his family's farm.

It was an ordinary enough tale, nothing glamorous or particularly exciting, but Miss Lewis had a way of making the past come to life with her words, and Pauline emerged from each session with the feeling she had stepped back in time and herself lived through the occurrences related by the elderly woman.

Today Miss Lewis had reminisced about the difficult years after her fiancé's death, how she struggled to find meaning and purpose to her life, how her father wanted her to return home, but she wanted something more. She had left it there, and Pauline was breathless with anticipation to discover what she did next.

"I think you do it on purpose," she said.

"Do what?" Miss Lewis asked.

"Break off at an exciting part each time. You do it ensure I'll keep coming back, so I can hear the next installment. You don't have to worry, you know. By now wild horses couldn't drag me away."

Miss Lewis laughed in a pleased fashion. "You flatter me, my dear! I can't imagine anything exciting in my life. I still feel it's somewhat presumptuous on my part to even want my story written down, but somehow, I can't bear the thought of no one remembering anything about Mother, or Tom, after I'm gone. My brothers and sisters never had a clear memory of our mother, you know, and Tom was an only child. If I had had children to pass my stories down to, maybe I wouldn't mind so much, but as it is, I take some comfort in knowing their memories will carry on even after I'm gone."

Pauline swallowed a sudden lump in her throat. She had never been interested in marrying, but the older woman's words did convey a sense of the loneliness of a lifetime lived on one's own.

"Enough of this," Miss Lewis said briskly. "How about a cup of tea before you go, dear?"

She said this every time, and every time, Pauline smiled and accepted. She didn't care very much for tea, but she had said "yes" the first time out of politeness, and now it had become something of a ritual.

She enjoyed watching Miss Lewis prepare the brew. First she brought the kettle to a boil while she washed out the flowered china teapot. Then she poured the boiling water into the pot to warm it while setting out the two delicate teacups and adding a cookie from her always-filled tin to each saucer.

Once the pot was warmed, Miss Lewis emptied it, added the fragrant black leaves, filled it once again with boiling water, turned her three-minute hourglass over, set the fine wire mesh tea strainer over the first teacup, and at last, when the three minutes were up, poured the tea.

It was an elaborate process, and it put Pauline in mind of stories she had heard of the Old World, and the ritual that afternoon tea had been in Victorian England. She appreciated this touch of European elegance in her life, and in truth, the flavor of the tea wasn't so bad once one got over wishing it was coffee.

This cookie was molasses, much to Pauline's relief. Some days it was a peanut butter cookie, which took all her grace to eat without grimacing. Those were the days she had to hurry home and eat an apple or drink a glass of milk, anything to rid herself of that cloying taste and feel in her mouth.

Today she was happy to linger over the tea, looking out the kitchen window at Miss Lewis's garden. Mostly vegetables, there were occasional bursts of color and bloom from various types of old-fashioned flowers: sweet peas, peonies, delphiniums, sweet-smelling lavender, and of course roses.

"It is so peaceful here," Pauline said, a trace of wistfulness in her voice.

Miss Lewis smiled gently as she followed Pauline's gaze. "Yes, it is a pleasant home. Small, of course, but I don't need it any larger for myself. I always knew I wanted my home to feel like a haven. I'm glad to hear you feel I've succeeded."

Pauline's thoughts flew to the small apartment she shared with her friend Sarah in town. They had no complaints of it, save for the tiring trek up the outside staircase to get to it on days they were weary, but neither did Pauline think it could be described as a haven. Perhaps there was more to the art of homemaking than she had always thought.

"Tell me, did you buy this house or build it?" she asked, more to make conversation than out of genuine curiosity.

Miss Lewis sat up straighter. "Oh, I'm so glad you asked! I had it built to my exact specifications, oh, fifteen years ago. Until then I'd always lived in other people's houses, and I wanted something that no one else had ever lived in, that was for me and me alone. My brother told me I was a fool to choose a piece of land so close to the County Home, but lands' sake, it's not those folks' fault they ended up in the poorhouse! And I must say I've never had a lick of trouble from any of them, just the occasional escaped chicken that tries to get into my garden."

Pauline laughed along with her hostess, but experienced a twinge of shame. Miss Lewis's house was separated from the County Home, known more colloquially as the poorhouse, by a large field and a row of trees, but even so, Pauline would have thought twice before building so close to society's outcasts. She thought of herself as a thoroughly modern, broad-minded woman, but this elderly retired schoolteacher had far more grace and compassion than she did.

"Yes," Miss Lewis said, still gazing unseeingly out the window. "I've been very happy here, and I'm thankful for it. Would you care for a tour, Miss Gray?"

Pauline set her teacup down carefully on its saucer. "That is most kind, thank you."

Again, she acted out of politeness, to please Miss Lewis, and again she reaped an unexpected reward. Up until this point Pauline had never seen more than the back porch and the kitchen. She had lived long enough in this rural area to know better than to enter by way of the front door! Miss Lewis had offered to conduct the interviews more formally, in the living room, but Pauline had fallen in love with this small, apple-green kitchen dominated by the gleaming, highly polished woodstove, and had firmly stated that she much preferred to sit at the table.

Now she saw how much she had missed in the rest of the house. The kitchen opened into the tiny dining room, which was papered in a soft marbled gold. The air was filled with a sweet scent of the pink roses in an old knobby jug sitting on a lace table runner on the table in the center of the room. The four chairs surrounding it had carved tops and moss green upholstered seats to match the drapes that frame the lace-curtained at the windows. In one corner of the room was a whatnot, its triangular shelves filled with curious objects. Pauline's attention was particularly drawn to the pair of Delftware candlesticks on the top shelf, as well as the green glass perfume bottle overlaid with silver filigree on the next shelf down. The detail of the filigree was exquisite.

"Mementos from my grandfather," Miss Lewis said. "He captained a merchant ship that went up and down the St. Lawrence. He always brought back something special for his children—my mother and her brother. After Mother's death my father wanted to destroy them—grief takes some people that way, you know. They can't bear to have anything left to remind them of their loss. I hid these in the attic until the day I could display them openly in my own home."

Miss Lewis picked up a photograph in a heavy silver frame from the next shelf. "This is a photo of a class picnic from one of my final years teaching," she said, handing it to Pauline.

The small, grainy, sepia faces meant little to Pauline, but she examined them out of politeness. "Very nice," she said.

Miss Lewis pointed to one of the figures. "That's Inez Grant—what a handful she was! And there next to her is Catherine Baker, the quietest and shyest student in her year. That's always the way of it, isn't it? The quiet ones are always drawn to the confident ones."

Pauline looked again. Inez Grant had her head thrown back in a laugh, and her arm was linked with a young man on one side, who looked down at her with obvious adoration. The Baker girl, on her other side, was a heavyset young woman with a scowl on what little of her face was visible through the hanging curtain of hair obscuring her features.

"Endless stories in every individual," she commented, handing the photo back.

She followed her hostess through the arched doorway into the living room, where she beheld an elegant wood-burning fireplace, two cast iron andirons shaped like owls glaring at her out of amber glass eyes from within.

"Charming, aren't they?" Miss Lewis asked with a chuckle, followed Pauline's line of sight. "Those were supposed to be a wedding gift from my Aunt Lillian, but when Tom passed away she gave them to me anyway. Said I should set them up when I had my own home, and so I did!"

Pauline had been startled by them at first, but now that she'd recovered she did have to admit they had a certain puckish charm to them.

The rest of the living room was simply but comfortably furnished with a low sofa and two wing-backed chairs with matching brocade upholstery. Cut flowers from Miss Lewis's garden sat in crystal vases on the polished wood side tables. A window seat with rose-spattered chintz cushions set into the bow window beckoned Pauline as a good spot to curl up and dream.

"You'll like this next room, Miss Gray," Miss Lewis said as they entered the central hall. She reached for the door handle to the last room on the first floor. "The builders wanted to make it another bedroom, but, goodness, I said, one bedroom for me and one for a guest is all I will ever need. This room is my sanctuary."

She opened the door, and Pauline beheld a vision.

"Mercy," she said once she'd regained her breath. "I've never seen so many books outside a library."

Miss Lewis laughed quietly. "I've been collecting them for a long time."

Aside from windows and the doorway, all four walls featured built-in bookcases filled with books. A wingback chair was placed in one corner, with a small round table next to it holding a reading lamp. A large wooden desk was set beneath the window looking into the back garden, making this the perfect room for reading or for writing.

"I had dreams of writing myself when I was younger," Miss Lewis said, her faded blue eyes going dreamy as her thoughts ranging back over the past. "But I never had the right touch. I can tell a story well enough, but somehow or other it loses all its zest when I write it down. That's why I'm so glad we have been able to collaborate, my dear. You are able to provide the writing skill my little life story requires."

"I must admit, if I had known this room was here I might never have gotten started on writing," Pauline said, eyes roaming over what titles she could see from her vantage point.

Miss Lewis laughed again. "Feel free to take anything home with you that you'd like! My library is open to all. You'd be amazed at how many boys and girls, housewives and farmers, students and workers alike have come out of this room with a book that captured their imagination. All I've asked in return is that if they find a book somewhere in their house that no one is interested in, they bring it to me to fill out my shelves. You'd be surprised at what I've received that way!"

"Wherever did you collect most of these?" Pauline said, taking Miss Lewis at her word and walking into the room to browse the shelves.

"Auctions and estate sales for many of them. Bookshops for others. Former students giving me books as a gift—so thoughtful, all of them. And, as I said, people bringing me their family's unwanted books. I had one farmer bring me a complete set of Dickens, if you can believe it! He said they'd been taking up room in their house for years and it was time they went to someone who would read them. You can imagine my delight.

"Oh yes, books and flowers. I let the neighborhood children pick flowers out of my garden to take home to their mothers, you see. They do the weeding that my arthritic hands can't manage anymore." Miss Lewis looked ruefully at her gnarled fingers. "That's the way to get through life, Miss Gray. Give what you can to others, and allow them to give to you when you have need."

Pauline's motto was more along the lines of "take care of oneself and never be beholden to anyone," but she thought Miss Lewis's way was, perhaps, the better.

After carefully tucking *Barchester Towers* and *Cranford* into her basket alongside a nosegay of roses and campanula, Pauline turned to her hostess, who always accompanied her to the front gate, and said a final thank-you.

Miss Lewis laughed. "Thank you, Miss Gray! I'm delighted to think of you enjoying those books."

As she always did, she opened her mailbox while Pauline mounted her bicycle, and checked to see if Al Denney, the mailman, had left her anything interesting. Today, she pulled out a long, slim white envelope and looked it over with interest.

"Well, I declare. I wonder who this could be? The handwriting doesn't look familiar..." She slipped her spectacles, which she wore on a chain around her neck, onto the bridge of her nose, carefully hooking the arms behind her ears. "Let's see, the return address says Miss Janet Arden. Well now... I wonder..."

Pauline left her still musing over the writer of the letter and began her ride back home. This ride was another source of enjoyment: the river flowed softly on one side of the road and there were only a few scattered houses on the other to interfere with the view of rolling fields and woods.

Pauline passed Miss Lewis's closest neighbor, a large, boxy red brick house with none of the charm and warmth of Miss Lewis's small home, waved courteously to the house's owner standing in her garden peering out into the road, and pondered who could have written Miss Lewis's mystery letter.

An old student? A relative? A relative of her fiancé? A childhood friend, likewise unmarried? The daughter of an old friend?

Not that it mattered in the long run! Pauline simply couldn't help turning over puzzles and attempting to make the pieces fit. At least this mystery was a small, harmless one, unlike some that she had solved.

She dismissed it from her mind until she had more information and set herself to wholly enjoying the ride back home.

CHAPTER TWO
Needles and Tongues

Pauline longed to dive into the newly-borrowed books as soon as she reached the small, second-story apartment on Pleasant Street she and her friend Sarah called home, but duty's voice was stronger. Ruby Richardson—who had been Ruby Ferris before her recent marriage to police lieutenant James Richardson—was expecting a baby come winter, and the women of the Episcopal Church were gathering together to help her prepare. Pauline could neither sew nor knit well, and she pitied any baby forced to wear something she had crafted, but friendship meant she ought to at least show up. Perhaps she could hem a blanket or something equally dull.

In truth, Pauline was pleased to have been included in the gathering. She was not a Canton native, having first come there to attend St. Lawrence University and then staying on afterward when she fell in love with the town. Often she felt on the outskirts of things, always the outsider looking in. It was partially her own fault, for she knew her natural reserve and discomfort in society came across as being aloof and disdainful. It bothered her, but—if she was honest—not enough for her to change her ways.

It took her an embarrassingly long time to find her thimble, but at last Pauline stepped back outside the apartment, locking the door carefully behind her, and walked down the creaking wooden steps and down the street toward the towering gray stone church building.

Canton was at its prettiest right now, in early June. Flowers nodded and smiled from every front yard and window box, the trees all wore their daintiest and freshest green and yellow topcoats, and sunlight sifted over everything, turning even the peeling paint on the dingiest clapboards soft and gentle. Pauline walked briskly, enjoying the warmth on her bare arms and uncovered head. She ought to have worn a hat, especially for going to church, but she supposed the omission could be excused as the sewing circle was meeting in the basement.

Pauline took one last deep breath of the faintly-scented wind before entering the church and taking the stairs to the large, dimly-lit basement. She wished they could have met outside, but likely even the staidest and most responsible of matrons would have had a difficult time focusing on her stitches under a clear blue June sky.

"Oh Miss Gray, so glad you could join us," said Mrs. Rev. Hansen. Knowing Pauline's lack of skill from previous gatherings, she handed her a plain baby gown to hem and steered her to a seat closest to a window, with the best light. "We weren't sure you would be able to come."

"Have you been writing anything interesting for your column lately?" inquired one of the other ladies.

Pauline stifled the desire to reply, "No, only dull things," and instead said, "Actually, most recently I've been working on a rather fascinating private project. Miss Anita Lewis has asked me to help her compile her memoirs, so that her stories might not be forgotten after she is gone. For having lived such a quiet life, it certainly has been a full one."

"Oh yes," said Mrs. Hansen. "She did say something about that to me a few weeks ago after the service. Well, I'm glad you are doing that, Miss Gray. Miss Lewis must be full of stories, not just about her family but about all her students. I think most of us in this room were taught by her at one point or another, isn't that right, ladies?"

There was a murmur of agreement as heads nodded over the stitching.

"Were you?" Pauline asked, wondering if their memories of Miss Lewis might make an interesting counterpoint to her memories of them. "We haven't gotten to her teaching days yet. She just finished telling me about the death of her fiancé this morning, and how she looked for meaningful work to fill her life after he passed."

"Oh yes," said one of the older women there. "Tom Martens, poor chap. Mrs. Ingersoll, you live on his farm now, don't you?"

A sharp-faced woman who looked to be in her early forties nodded. "Hank's father bought it at auction and passed it to Hank and me when we married ten years later. It's a good farm: good land, solid house."

"Such a shame Tom died when he did," the older woman continued. "He and Anita were so in love. She seemed to just shrink into herself after he died, and it wasn't until she took up teaching that she came to life again. She poured herself into the children who came through her classroom, every one of them."

"I know I wouldn't have made it past sixth grade without her help in mathematics," agreed Mrs. Hansen. "Mrs. Addison, didn't she help you with one of your subjects as well?"

A quiet, dark-haired woman Pauline hadn't met before now raised her head from the corner where she had been diligently working at trimming a baby bonnet. "Oh yes," she said. "All of them. I was quite the dunce. My parents didn't consider education necessary for women, and so I got no encouragement at home. If it hadn't been for Miss Lewis, I wouldn't even be able to read or write today."

Mrs. Ingersoll clicked her tongue. "Miss Lewis never did approve of ignorance for anyone, no matter what the parents said. Do you remember how she confronted old Dave Billings, who sneered his boys as sissies whenever he caught them reading?"

A ripple of laughter ran around the room. "Drove her old buggy out to his farm after school and called *him* a few names!" another woman said. "Told him that just because he grew up an ignorant old coot was no reason his sons should suffer the same fate. By the end of it, she had him agreeing to learn to read just so's he could keep up with his sons—and she kept him to that promise. Drove out once a week to check on him, see if he was making progress, bring him fresh materials. Changed his entire life, she did, and his sons' lives as well. Old Dave grew devoted to books, and both his boys went on to college, and the youngest is a professor at a university out west somewhere."

"Oh heavens," Mrs. Hansen added, looking at Pauline, who had long since abandoned the baby gown. "You aren't taking notes on this, Miss Gray?"

Pauline blushed and tucked the notebook and pencil back into her handbag. "Forgive me—it was so interesting I forgot myself. Don't worry, I would never publish anything without permission."

"Goodness, young lady, if you find anything I say worth repeating, do so with my blessing!" said Mrs. Ingersoll. "Nobody's ever cared so much about my ramblings before."

"I begin to think everyone has a wealth of stories hidden away inside them," Pauline said, wincing as she stabbed herself with the needle, trying not to drip blood on the tiny gown.

"I suppose that's true," Mrs. Hansen agreed thoughtfully. "Only some folk would rather theirs stay inside instead of bringing them out into the light of day."

"There are a few things in my past I'd rather others not know," agreed the woman who had told about Dave Billings. "We all have our secrets as well as our stories."

The woman who had called herself a dunce—Mrs. Addison—shook her head. "Not me. My life is an open book. A dull one," she added with a laugh that sounded something like a sigh.

"Now, Mrs. Addison, that's not true!" chided one of the others. "I'm sure you have plenty of stories tucked away, just like the rest of us."

"If Miss Gray is writing Miss Lewis's memoirs, I suppose some of our stories will come out, too," chuckled Mrs. Ingersoll. "I hope none of you ladies have any dark misdeeds in your youth that you want hidden!"

It was a joke, but an awkward silence fell over the room all the same.

"I'm sure Miss Lewis would never betray a trust," Mrs. Hansen said into the silence.

"Isn't that a great deal to ask of anyone, though?" one of the other women said. "I don't know that I'd want to trust any of my secrets—if I had any—to another person, no matter how dependable."

"Best not to have any secrets at all!" Mrs. Ingersoll said with another chuckle. "We should all be so lucky as Cathy here."

Mrs. Addison smiled again faintly, but made no other answer.

"Secrets can be poisonous things," Mrs. Hansen said. "Best to live in such a way that you aren't ashamed to have your past shown up in the light of day."

That may have been good Christian reasoning, but it wasn't the most comforting for everyone, based on the closed expressions on many of the women's faces. Pauline decided it was up to her to give some reassurance. "We can change names if anyone is uncomfortable with any stories told about them. Besides, Miss Lewis seems more interested in sharing her memories of her family and fiancé than in revealing youthful peccadilloes of her students."

"Thank heaven for that!" Mrs. Ingersoll said with an exaggerated sigh of relief, and the tension broke on a general wave of laughter as the conversation turned back to Ruby and James Richardson and speculation as to whether they were going to have a boy or a girl, and what he or she would be named, and how young Jeremy, Ruby's twelve-year-old son from her first marriage, would feel about a much younger sibling.

As the gathering ended, Pauline found herself leaving the building in the company of the dark-haired woman—Mrs. Addison—and Klara Hertz, sister to Heinrich and Margret Berger, who ran a laundry service out of their home.

Miss Hertz—shorter than Pauline and older by ten years or so, with her graying hair braided and wound around her head—smiled cheerfully at the other two. "So enjoyable, to spend an afternoon sewing together for another. It is far better than trying to work in a kitchen full of dripping clothes, listening to Heinrich's old truck rattle and wheeze in and out of the yard as he delivers and collects!"

Pauline laughed with her. "I am afraid my sewing skills mean this poor baby is going to have at least one gown coming apart at the seams, but I agree, it is better than sitting at home by myself."

To her surprise, she meant it. Though it had been difficult to tear herself away from her books and typewriter, this outing had done her good. It was pleasant to be part of a community, and to know that if she were ever in need, these women would come together to help her just as they did for each other.

"I enjoy the chance to escape the kitchen as well," said Mrs. Addison. "And a different sort of sewing than the never-ending mending that comes from three small boys!"

"Ach, you would miss it if it weren't there," said Miss Hertz.

Mrs. Addison smiled. "I suppose I would. We mothers like to grumble, but really, there's nothing I wouldn't do for my boys." A new light shone in her eyes, and for a moment Pauline could almost picture her as a Valkyrie, or Brunhilde.

Pauline's mother had been the sort who continually sighed over how disappointing her children were. Pauline wondered what it would be like to have grown up with a mother ready to take any steps to defend and protect her family instead. On the one hand, it seemed comforting. On the other, without her mother's all-too-obvious dissatisfaction in her daughter, would Pauline have ever had the impetus to leave home and pursue a life of her own?

Her thoughts were interrupted by a commotion down the street, and she turned to see young Officer Wallace approaching the church with his hand wrapped firmly around the upper arm of a squirming, protesting youngster.

Mrs. Addison let out a heart-rending cry. "Mikey!" She ran forward just as the boy succeeded in pulling away from Officer Wallace and dashing to his mother.

"It wasn't me, Ma, I didn't do it," he whined.

Mrs. Addison wrapped him in a hug, then stood to confront Officer Wallace. Pauline's impression of her as a

Valkyrie in defense of her children hadn't been far off—with her arms akimbo and her chin jutting out, she looked ready to tear poor Wallace from limb to limb.

"Officer, what is the meaning of this? How dare you manhandle my poor boy?"

Wallace ran a finger around the inside of his collar, but stood his ground. "He kept trying to run away, ma'am. I was worried he would get run over by an auto or a cyclist or trampled by a horse."

Mrs. Addison cried out again and wrapped one arm around young Mikey's shoulders. "My baby! But what were you doing that made him so frightened of you that he wanted to run away?"

"I caught him throwing mud at the mayor's auto, parked outside the Opera House, ma'am," Wallace said. "When I told him to stop, he tried to run away. I just wanted to get him safely to you so you could handle the matter."

"I didn't do it," Mikey said again, the whine still present in his voice.

Pauline trusted Officer Wallace, but even if she hadn't, she would have doubted Mikey's veracity. For one thing, there was mud all over the sides of his short pants where he had rubbed his hands to clean them. Beside her, Miss Hertz clicked her tongue.

"Those boys!" she said softly. "Always in trouble, and their mother never does a thing to control them."

"I'll thank you to leave my sons alone from now on, Officer, and not make false accusations," Mrs. Addison bit out. "Of course Mikey wouldn't do a thing like that! For shame."

Pauline couldn't stand there and see Wallace made the victim of a false accusation. She started forward, intending to point out the mud on Mikey's clothes, but Miss Hertz placed a hand on her shoulder and stopped her.

"It will do no good," she whispered, shaking her head. "She will only become angry at you as well."

Wallace stepped back. "I'm not making accusations, ma'am, just stating what I saw. The mayor won't be happy about the state of his automobile, but that's your responsibility now. Good day." He tipped his hat with an exaggerated air of politeness, and walked away.

Mrs. Addison looked back, seemingly aware of her audience for the first time. She blushed deeply and hurried off, Mikey's hand in hers, without a word of goodbye.

"Poor Cathy," said Mrs. Ingersoll, joining Miss Hertz and Pauline. "Her own parents were so strict with her, never let her have a moment's peace, always sure that she was doing wrong even when she wasn't. Now she's gone the other way with her lads, and won't hear a word against them, even for ordinary boyish escapades."

"That is not good child-raising," Miss Hertz said. "Either one."

Mrs. Ingersoll nodded. "I always felt so badly for Cathy when we were girls, but she was hard to befriend, always so quiet. Not like me!" She laughed. "I was always in the center of a crowd. Not too good for my grades, but it did make my school years more fun." She winked roguishly at Pauline. "My parents probably ought to have been a little stricter with me sometimes! I know they despaired sometimes that I'd ever pick just one of my beaus and settle down." She laughed again. "And now here I am, a staid farmer's wife with a thickening waistline and two sons of my own. My younger self would be horrified!"

Miss Hertz shook her head once more, but she was smiling. "You Americans!"

Mrs. Ingersoll chuckled. "Well, well. I am thankful for Miss Lewis. I could have ended up far wilder in my youth if she hadn't taken a hand. She took Cathy under her wing as well, though in a different way. I think she made Cathy feel... safe. That was her gift, you know. She always saw just what each student needed, and provided it for them."

These words made Pauline look forward even more to the next memoir session with Miss Lewis. Not only for the unfolding story, but for the gentle companionship of the wise and kindly woman who was telling it.

CHAPTER THREE
Murder

The next two days passed uneventfully: Pauline typed up her notes from Miss Lewis; forced herself to work further on her current Emma Daring novel; made uninspiring meals for herself; kept the apartment reasonably tidy; and enjoyed her novels from Miss Lewis's library. With Sarah away visiting family downstate, Pauline managed to pass both days without speaking with a single soul save Heinrich Berger when he stopped by to collect the linens for his wife to wash. Hence, she was even more eager for company than she had anticipated as she cycled out of the village, following the course of the Grasse River until she reached the white cottage with the rose bushes in front.

But there was an unexpected addition to the front of the house: a black Ford Model T parked by the roses. Pauline skidded to a stop and nearly fell off her bicycle as she recognized the insignia of the Canton Police Department on the side of the car.

What on earth were the police doing at Miss Lewis's?

Through force of will, Pauline ignored the nervous churning in her stomach at this hint of trouble. She carefully leaned the bicycle up against the fence, took off her gloves to wipe her suddenly perspiring palms on her handkerchief, replaced the gloves, and walked around to the back to knock on the kitchen door as usual.

Her path along the garden walkway was interrupted by big, burly, blond-haired Lieutenant James Richardson erupting from the back door to intercept her, bringing with him the scent of freshly-baked bread.

"Pauline!" he exclaimed. "For crying out loud, don't tell me the *Times* has put you onto this just because you're closest? How did they hear about it so quickly, anyway?"

The dread in Pauline's stomach solidified into an icy lump. She had to swallow twice before she could speak. "I am here for my usual appointment with Miss Lewis," she said. "I'm working with her to write her memoirs. Is she all right? Was it a robbery? May I see her?" She hadn't realized just how fond she had become of the elderly woman until there was a promise of danger to her.

James's face grew somber. "That's right, I'd forgotten about that. I'm darned sorry to have to tell you this, Pauline. Miss Lewis was killed last night."

The garden, James, and the back of the cottage all swirled together in front of Pauline's face. She had the vague idea James said something else, but the buzzing in her ears was so loud she couldn't hear him.

Then the nausea grew more intense, and she knew she was going to disgrace herself by being ill.

She barely felt James steadying her, guiding her to sit down on the garden bench and put her head between her knees.

"Deep breaths," she dimly heard him say. "Easy, there. Nice and slow. Breathe."

She focused on her breathing, in and out, slow and steady, and eventually her stomach settled enough for her to dare lifting her head. James was squatting on his heels in front of her, his good-natured face concerned.

"I sent Wallace next door to ask for a glass of water for you," he said. "He should be back at any moment. I'd get you one here, but..." He shrugged helplessly. "It is a crime scene."

"I apologize," Pauline said, embarrassment now mixing with her physical discomfort. "I should not be taking your attention at this time, when you should be free to focus on—on Miss Lewis." She stopped and pressed her lips together, unable to say anything more.

"Gosh, it's not your fault, Pauline," James said. "I shouldn't have broken it to you like that, should've eased into it, had you sit down first or something. You didn't ask for this."

Young Officer Wallace, his red hair a flame against the pale blue sky, hurried back into the garden with a tumbler of water in hand, followed by a short, plump woman, talking busily away.

"... well I knew something was wrong, of course, seeing you all here, and I was worried sick for Miss Lewis, but I never would have guessed it was this bad if you hadn't come over—and I must say I do think her neighbors ought to have been told first, not that it's any of my business, but if there's a madman out there we all ought to know to protect ourselves and—oh, Miss Gray, I'm so sorry, I know how much Miss Lewis was enjoying remembering her past with you—oh, hello, Officer—oh, Lieutenant? I always thought that was military—oh, police as well? Well, Lieutenant, when this young man told me that Miss Gray needed some water because she almost fainted, I knew I had to come right over. You policemen are very good at solving crimes and keeping us safe— though you didn't keep Miss Lewis safe, but I suppose that you can't be everywhere all the time—but you aren't very good at taking care of people. Miss Gray, you come right over to my house and rest on my sofa until you're ready to get yourself home."

Pauline hadn't met this woman before, but she supposed Miss Lewis must have told her neighbor about the memoir and Pauline's role in the project. There was genuine kindness in this woman's face, even if it was tempered by avid curiosity. That was unavoidable, she supposed.

In any case, she couldn't continue to sit here distracting James from his job. She sipped at the cool water, feeling life flush back into her cheeks and down to her hands and feet.

"Thank you, ma'am," she said quietly. "James, will you need to speak to me before I return home?"

"It might be necessary," he said, helping her to her feet and keeping a steadying hand under her elbow. "Once we've finished here I'll come see you at Mrs....?"

"MacNeill, Mrs. Amy MacNeill," that woman supplied.

"Mrs. MacNeill's," James said. "And we'll give you a ride back. Wallace can bring your bicycle."

Pauline would have protested, but common sense told her she would not be fit to ride her bicycle after this—she would be a danger to herself and anyone she met on the road. She nodded. "Very well."

Officer Wallace looked unhappy, but didn't complain.

"We will need to ask you some questions as well, Mrs. MacNeill, about anything you might have heard or seen last night or early this morning," James told the neighbor woman.

"Anything I can do to help," Mrs. MacNeill said. "Poor Miss Lewis!"

She put an arm around Pauline's waist and steered her along the path out of the garden and toward the large white farmhouse on the other side of the fence, talking the entire way.

"Goodness sake, you poor thing, you must just feel dreadful. Did the police officer—that lieutenant—did he say anything about how it happened? That young red-headed one only told me Miss Lewis was killed. Dear, dear... was it a burglar? That lieutenant said they'd be asking me questions, but I didn't hear anything at all last night. Oh dear, you don't think they think I had anything to do with it? That would be dreadful!"

By the time she was seated on the stiff horsehair sofa in Mrs. MacNeill's front room, Pauline's head was throbbing.

"I'm afraid I really don't know anything more than you do, ma'am," she managed to say.

"Oh, of course not, of course you don't. Although I did wonder, since you seem to be on first-name basis with that policeman..." Mrs. MacNeill let the statement trail off suggestively while her eyes went to Pauline's still-gloved hands, rather too obviously searching for the shape of a wedding band.

Pauline held back a groan. Would people ever leave off assuming she and James were romantically inclined toward each other? Of all the nonsense in the world, that which insisted men and women could not simply be friends was the worst.

"Lieutenant Richardson and I are old friends," she said as firmly as she could under the circumstances. "His wife is also a good friend of mine."

"Oh yes, I see. I *thought* Miss Lewis had referred to you as a miss, not a missus," said Mrs. MacNeill, nodding as she seemingly slotted Pauline into her proper place in her mind. What category was that, Pauline wondered: hopeless spinster? Crossed in love? Waiting for the right man?

Bluestocking was the one Pauline heard the most frequently. It fit better than the others, though truly, she did dislike categories.

Mrs. MacNeill plumped herself down in the upholstered chair across from the couch, fanning her face with her hand. Her endless stream of chatter slowed as the reality of the situation seeped in.

"Dear, dear me. You could have knocked me over with a feather, you honestly could have, Miss Gray, when the policeman told me what happened. The milkman's the one who found her, you know, as he was dropping off the milk. I peeked out my window—not that I'm nosy, you know, but one does wonder when the milk is late, and when one sees the truck next door and it doesn't leave and doesn't leave. Well, the next thing I knew the police had showed up, and then I really started to wonder, and then they finally let him go along the rest of his round, and of course I had to ask him what had happened, and he told me he wasn't allowed to talk about it but that something dreadful had happened to Miss Lewis, and then..." She sniffed and dabbed at her eyes with a clean handkerchief. "Then that young policeman came over to ask me for a glass of water for you, and I made him tell me just what had happened, and oh *dear*. She was such a lovely person, and the best neighbor I could have asked for. Oh, it doesn't seem right that she should be killed!"

That was exactly it. It wasn't right; it was all wrong. No one deserved death, but there were some for whom it felt especially wrong, and this was a violent death of some sort. Pauline didn't know how it happened, or who had done it, but a fierce determination swelled in her breast to find justice for Miss Lewis.

"I'm so sorry, Mrs. MacNeill," she said, seeing the other woman as a person for the first time. "I only knew her a little, but you were her friend. As painful as this is for me, it must be worse for you."

Mrs. MacNeill leaned forward and patted her knee. "That's a kind thing to say, Miss Gray."

It was? Perhaps Pauline was getting better at interacting with people.

"Miss Lewis did so enjoy your sessions," Mrs. MacNeill continued. "You brought her youth back to her. She would come over to bring me a bunch of flowers most days, and she always had an extra sparkle in her eyes the days you visited. Even if you weren't able to complete her memoirs, you did a good thing for her, just letting her remember."

Pauline's throat closed. "Thank you," she managed.

Conversation dwindled after that, and it was with relief that both women saw James and Wallace finally leave the Lewis cottage and approach Mrs. MacNeill's front door.

"Of course they would come to the front, rather than to the back like civilized people," Mrs. MacNeill grumbled under her breath as she jumped up to wrestle open the big green door.

James ducked his head as he entered, his hat in his hands. "Ma'am," he said.

Officer Wallace slipped in behind him, an anxious shadow.

"Officer—I mean Lieutenant," Mrs. MacNeill said, "Please, what can you tell me about Miss Lewis's—" she swallowed— "death?"

James shook his head. "I can't release much information yet, ma'am."

Mrs. MacNeill sat back down, frustration and fear evident on her face. Pauline leaned forward. It was her turn to do a kindness for the other woman.

"Lieutenant Richardson, could you at least let Mrs. MacNeill know if she should have someone to stay with her for the next few nights? Is she likely to be in danger?"

Mrs. MacNeill cast her a grateful glance, while James frowned thoughtfully.

"It might be just as well if you did, ma'am," he said at last. "You understand we can't confirm anything, but as of right now, evidence points to this being a burglary gone wrong. You didn't see or hear anything last night?"

Mrs. MacNeill shook her head. "Not that I can remember. What—what time?"

"It would have been before she went to bed, based on, er, based on her clothing," James said. "And that is absolutely all I can say," he added firmly.

It was Pauline's turn to frown. Something about that didn't ring true, but what? She hadn't even seen the scene for herself, so why did it sound wrong?

Mrs. MacNeill thought, then shook her head one more time. "I wish I could say yes, Lieutenant, but I don't remember suspicious—wait! Someone did stop by yesterday evening, but it wasn't a burglar. And he couldn't have been the—the killer, because I heard him say 'good-night' to Miss Lewis when he left. It must have been her nephew, because he said, 'Good night, Aunt Anita.'" She stopped triumphantly.

James looked at Officer Wallace, and then over at Pauline. She nodded. She'd picked up on the discrepancy as well.

"Did you hear Miss Lewis reply, or see her?" James asked gently.

Mrs. MacNeill considered it. "No, but it wasn't as though I was snooping," she said. "I'm not a nosy neighbor. I was simply out admiring the sunset when he left." She folded her arms across her bosom.

"I see." James pulled out his notepad and pencil and wrote something down. "Thank you, Mrs. MacNeill. I think that's all for right now. Do you have someone you can ask to come stay with you for a night or two?"

"Oh yes, my son will come by, and he'll bring his dog. I'll be perfectly safe, thank you."

"Then we'll say good-bye for now. Pauline, are you ready?"

Pauline rose to her feet and was pleased to find herself perfectly steady. She probably could have cycled home, were it not for the likelihood that James wanted to talk with her.

"Quite, thank you. Mrs. MacNeill, I am so grateful for your kindness."

"Not at all, Miss Gray. I only wish we could have met under better circumstances."

After a few more platitudes, Pauline and James got themselves settled in the police car, and Officer Wallace unhappily mounted the bicycle and wobbled off down the road.

"All right," James said with a sigh, releasing the brake and engaging the motor. "We need to talk."

CHAPTER FOUR
Too Close to Home

"You think it was the nephew, not a random burglary gone wrong?" Pauline asked.

James kept his eyes on the road as he answered. "It's hard to say. The obvious thought is that someone from the County Home broke in hoping to find something worth stealing. The place was a mess—books strewn everywhere, papers scattered, knick-knacks all over the place, vases overturned and smashed—"

Pauline winced at the thought of the lovely house so torn apart. "I see."

"But," James continued. "Nothing valuable was taken. The silver's all still there, she had a tiny statue still on one shelf that is gilded with real gold, there are good pictures on the walls. So either Miss Lewis interrupted the burglar before he could take anything and he hit her over the head, then panicked and ran when he saw that he'd killed her, or it wasn't a burglary at all." He stopped short. "I shouldn't have told you that detail," he said. "Forget I said it, will you?"

Pauline was only too happy to push the thought of Miss Lewis's death from her mind. "If that's the case, why tear the house apart? Surely a burglar would take the obviously valuable things before ransacking a house, especially if he is so foolish as to come early in the night when his victim is still awake."

"Right," James said. "Not to mention the folks at the County Home are for the most part decent, law-abiding people, just down on their luck."

"Miss Lewis told me she had never had any problems with them as her neighbors," Pauline agreed.

James nodded. "So it looks almost as though the nephew must have done it when he was visiting, then made a mess to make it look like a burglary, and then pretended to be saying good night to his aunt as he left for the benefit of the clearly not-nosy-at-all Mrs. MacNeill."

Pauline had to smile at that description, though it was short-lived. "But why? Why would her nephew want to kill her?" She couldn't imagine why anyone would want to kill Miss Lewis, much less her own family.

James's profile was grim. "I'd say there's a good chance she's left him something substantial in her will. Maybe everything, who knows? That would explain why he didn't actually steal anything valuable, he didn't want to have to hide pieces of his own inheritance."

"That's appalling," Pauline said softly.

James flickered a quick glance at her before returning his attention to the road. "Murder usually is."

"Was that all you wished to discuss?" Pauline asked after a moment or two.

"Oh," said James. "Mostly. It helps to talk through things with another person, and Wallace, much as he's coming along, is far too inclined to blindly respond 'yes sir' to everything I say."

"I see." That was a cheering thought, that James valued her clear thinking enough to want to discuss the case with her.

"I also wanted to warn you to be careful. This is a dangerous person we are working against, and while I know you have had fine successes with a couple of other cases, I would feel much better if you would promise to stay out of this one."

"Ah."

Pauline's first instinct was to prickle up her feathers defensively. So, when James needed to talk through things, she was good enough to be included, but not for anything else? Was this because she had almost fainted? Did he think her too weak? How typically masculine!

Then reason intervened. James was *worried*, the same way she would be if a friend was getting involved in something dangerous. It was what friends did: they cared for each other and worried about each other. He wasn't dismissing her abilities.

"I can't promise that without reservations," Pauline said at last. "I won't be able to help thinking about it and mulling it over and trying to work it through in my mind. But I can promise you that I won't go about actively investigating, at least not without discussing it with you first."

James sighed and smiled at the same time. "I suppose that's the best I could hope for."

He pulled over to the side of the road by the tall, narrow, gray-clapboard building that was home to Pauline, though she had never, in all the years she had lived in the second-story apartment, felt anywhere near as at home there as she had during her few visits to Miss Lewis. She shivered, thinking of all that peace and graciousness, that kindly warmth, wiped out in a moment by someone consumed with greed or anger.

James noted her tremor as he opened the car door for her. "I'd better come up with you, just to make sure you don't lose your balance on the stairs," he said.

Pauline offered him an embarrassed smile. "I'm perfectly recovered now, but thank you. I feel rather a fool for losing my head earlier."

"Nonsense," he said, following her up the narrow wooden staircase that went up the outside of the house. "It would have been a shock for anyone. I shouldn't have dropped it on you so suddenly like that."

Any response Pauline would have made to that died on her lips as she reached her front door. She distinctly recalled locking it behind her as she left that morning. Now, it was slightly open, swinging in the gentle breeze, and there were shiny scratches around the keyhole on the dull metal plate.

"James," she managed to whisper.

He took one look past her shoulder and muttered a word under his breath that would have shocked Pauline any other time. "Get back down the stairs," he hissed, precariously squeezing past her.

Pauline opened her mouth to argue, then closed it again and retreated as told. Much as she would have liked to be able to boldly stride into her own home and confront whoever had broken in, she knew she did not have the physical strength to stand against a man who had already killed once—presuming this was the same person who had killed Miss Lewis, and anything else seemed far too coincidental for Pauline's brain to accept.

She waited at the bottom of the staircase, pulse thundering in her ears, while James slid through the open door and vanished inside her apartment. Almost immediately, she started wondering: how long should she wait for him to come out? What if something happened to him—how would she ever explain it to Ruby? Where was Mrs. Harper, Pauline's landlady and downstairs neighbor? Had anything happened to her?

Before she had time to work herself into a proper panic, James appeared at the door again. His face was grim.

"It's safe," he said. "But I should warn you that it isn't pretty."

Pauline didn't allow herself any more time to think. She ran up the wooden stairs. James stepped back to allow her inside. She set foot in the tiny foyer—and gasped.

It seemed as though all her books and papers had been pulled from their places and scattered across the entire apartment. Her typewriter was overturned; every drawer in her desk had been pulled all the way out and thrown onto the floor; even the newspaper had been torn in two.

"It's like this in the bedrooms as well," James said from behind her. He cleared his throat. "I, uh, I should apologize, I suppose, for going into your private rooms, but I had to make sure the thief was not still here."

"There's no privacy when a crime has been committed," Pauline said through numb lips.

"Nothing else has been touched," James continued after a brief moment. "Your clothing, jewelry, money... it's all been left untouched. The kitchen is fine. Only books and papers. Just like at Miss Lewis's."

Pauline couldn't seem to think. It was as though a heavy woolen blanket had pressed down over her brain. She fought past it. Before James had told her to come up, she had been worried about something. What was it?

She closed her eyes, and a spark of life returned. "James. Could you kindly check in on Mrs. Harper? I want to be sure she was not troubled by thieves as well."

James muttered yet another curse she didn't think she was supposed to have heard, and vanished. Pauline heard his boots on the stairs, thudding quickly from one step to the next.

Pauline forced herself to move further into her home—a safe haven no longer, the violence done here shaking her to her very core. Even if they cleaned it all up, even if they caught the intruder, she wasn't sure she'd ever be able to see this room without seeing this invasion.

Why? What could she have that was so important?

Another spark of life flickered through her brain. The novels she had borrowed from Miss Lewis—what if they were worth more than either woman had realized? What if the murderer had killed Miss Lewis for them, and then come after Pauline when he didn't find them in the house?

She waded through the sea of paper and, after some hunting, her heart hurting with every bent cover or torn page for each book she turned over, she found first *Cranford* and then *Barchester Towers*. Both books were facedown on the floors, their pages crumpled. The intruder hadn't missed them; he simply hadn't bothered about them.

That was one theory gone.

Still, Pauline reasoned that this intrusion had to be connected with Miss Lewis's murder. The similarity of the searches, the timing of it... whoever it was thought she had something that he had looked for and couldn't find at Miss Lewis's house.

She was sorting through papers on the floor, looking for her notes for the memoir, when James returned.

"Mrs. Harper is fine and—darn it, Pauline! You should know better than to interfere with a crime scene! We need to examine everything for fingerprints, hunt for clues, before you start tidying up."

Pauline sat back on her heels. She placed her hands on her flushed cheeks, embarrassed. "Oh dear. I'm sorry, James. I didn't think."

He relented, crossing the room to squat down beside her. "I suppose it's different when it affects you personally."

"Perhaps so, but it shouldn't be. One should always be able to hold to one's principles and keep one's head."

He flashed her a quick grin. "Yes, but one would be hardly human then, and not half so likable."

Some of the ice surrounding Pauline started to thaw at that. She almost managed a smile in return. "Was Mrs. Harper all right?"

"Yes, and I should warn you, she'll be up here shortly. She's not too happy about this, and very upset that I left you alone even to come speak with her. I think she's planning on offering you her guest room tonight, so if you'd rather not sleep with her, think of an excuse quickly."

"Oh," Pauline said. She hadn't even thought of sleeping arrangements.

"You know you're always welcome with us as well," James continued. "Ruby would scold me dreadfully if I told her I left you alone in your apartment after it had been burglarized."

Pauline produced another partial smile. "Thank you, you're very kind. I'll have to think it over, if you don't mind. Right now I can't seem to focus on anything except finding my notes from my sessions with Miss Lewis."

"Ah, so that's what you were doing!"

James examined the floor and sighed. "We'll have to check all these for fingerprints before we do anything else. That's a good thought, though—you put your finger right on the one thing connecting you and Miss Lewis."

"Miss Lewis, me, and paper," Pauline said. "Since it seems to be either paper or books or both that this person is after."

"Doesn't make sense, though," James said. "Surely you wouldn't have anything in your notes that you didn't also hear Miss Lewis say. So why take..." His voice trailed off.

Pauline looked at him curiously.

James swallowed and spoke again. "Actually, Pauline, I think I'd prefer it if you let me take you home to stay with Ruby and me tonight, and every night until we catch the fellow who did this."

It took Pauline's still-sluggish brain a few minutes to work this through. "Oh," she said at last. "Oh, you think there's something she might have told me and I wrote down, and oh." Her voice grew very small. "You think this person might try to kill me too because of what I know."

"It's far-fetched, but I don't like to take the chance," James said. "Unless there's something else she gave you or wrote to you that can make sense of any of this." He waved an arm to encompass the mess.

"Not right now," Pauline sighed. Nothing made sense to her at this moment.

James looked down at the paper nearest him on the floor. "Say, what's this? This looks like part of some story or something. Emma Daring—isn't that the heroine of those adventure novels? What are you doing with—"

Mrs. Harper entered the apartment at that moment, and Pauline had never been so thankful to see her landlady.

Not only had her home been violated and her privacy stripped away, now her greatest secret trembled on the brink of revelation.

CHAPTER FIVE
Suspicions

Mrs. Harper was voluble in her horror at the damage done to Pauline's property— "And with me in my kitchen the entire time, the wretches! I heard some noises above my head, but I thought it was Miss Gray returned from her outing. If only I'd looked out my window to see that your bicycle wasn't in its usual spot by the fence! Then I would have known something was wrong, and I could have come up and caught them in the act."

"Just as well you didn't," James said gravely. "Whoever it was is a dangerous person, Mrs. Harper. I'm thankful neither you nor Pauline were endangered by him."

That had the effect of silencing Mrs. Harper. Her eyes widened as the implications of James's statement sank in.

"Well," she finally gasped. "You'll sleep in my guest room tonight, dearie, and we'll lock all the doors and windows and put chairs beneath the doorknobs."

"Actually," James interposed, "my wife would like to have Pauline stay with us for a few nights. But locking your doors is a good plan regardless."

Mrs. Harper seemed inclined to bridle at the thought of the Richardsons taking over her lodger, but as Pauline showed no inclination one way or the other her indignation soon fizzled.

"And you didn't see anything helpful, Mrs. Harper?" James asked, escorting her to the door.

"Not a thing. I heard the paperboy earlier, and Mr. Berger delivering laundry—that old truck of his squeaks something awful—but other than that, nothing. My mind was taken up with getting the bread out of the oven and starting the roast for dinner and..."

"Thank you," James said firmly, opening the door.

Mrs. Harper reluctantly left, then popped her head back around. "I'll just bring you a slice of bread and butter and a glass of milk, shall I, Miss Gray? I'm sure you could use it."

Pauline wrenched her mind to the present. "Thank you, Mrs. Harper, I'd appreciate that."

In truth, she didn't think she could ever eat or drink again, but the logical part of her brain told her she would need to take nourishment or she would not be able to function at all.

"All my notes from Miss Lewis are gone," she told James as he closed the door behind her landlady.

"That settles it, then," he said. "The burglar was looking here for whatever he couldn't find at Miss Lewis's house. The question is, did he find it here, or is it still missing?"

"That's not the only question," Pauline said. "The bigger one is, what was it he was looking for?"

James sighed. "And here I was hoping to take Jeremy fishing this weekend. Listen, I need to report back to the Chief. We need someone here to take fingerprints, and I need to see if the doctor has any clearer idea of when Miss Lewis was killed. Once we're done fingerprinting in here and I've had a look around for any clues, you can pack an overnight bag and I'll take you home to Ruby."

Pauline shook her head. "James, I might as well tell you now, I have papers here I don't want anyone else to see. There's nothing wrong in them, but they are—" she hesitated, recalling what she had told him only a short time ago "—private."

"I am sorry," James said. "But you know I can't give you special privilege just because we're friends. The best I can do is promise that anything I see here that seems private, I'll do my best to ignore. It goes without saying that I won't tell anyone your secrets, of course."

Pauline knew that. Still, she hated to concede. There was nothing to be ashamed of in her novels, but she couldn't help it: she *was* ashamed of them. Ashamed that her lofty goals of scholarship when she graduated from St. Lawrence University— however vague they had been—had come down to writing cheap adventure novels without a lick of literary quality to recommend them.

Perhaps it was vanity, but she did not want to see the respect other people held for her diminished by the knowledge she wrote such drivel. Not even from James.

A stirring of anger broke through the numbness that had engulfed her from the moment she saw the desecration of her living space. How dare this person do this to her? It was bad enough he had made her feel unsafe in her own home, now he was continuing to injure her even from a distance.

For the first time, Pauline's desire for justice became personal, rather than an ideal.

She rose to her feet, dusting her hands on her skirt. "So be it," she said. "But I'd rather stay here and clean this place up after you leave. I understand that you don't want me to stay overnight here alone, but I can't leave my home in this condition." She gestured at the area around her. "If nothing else, I have a responsibility to Sarah to make sure nothing of hers was destroyed or damaged."

"We'll be here for quite some time, what with checking for fingerprints and footprints and any other physical evidence," James warned. "And I still don't like the idea of you wandering around town on your own. Someone was frightened enough of information you might or might not have to break into your place in broad daylight and ransack it. Who's to say they won't return, or try to attack you on your way out to our place?"

"Why would they return?" Pauline protested. "They had plenty of time to look for whatever it was they wanted when they were here before. There's no reason for them to come back. As for attacking me, that seems equally unlikely." She hesitated, unable to give a reason for why it would not be likely other than that the very notion sounded ridiculous. How many victims of robbery or murder thought the same, though? "I will telephone you when I am ready to leave so that someone can accompany me to your house."

James visibly wrestled with this for a few moments, then accepted her compromise. "If you insist."

Mrs. Harper returned then with a slice of bread on a delicate plate with roses around the perimeter, clearly the good china rather than her everyday ware. Pauline inhaled the warm, comforting scent, and her hunger rose unexpectedly.

"This looks delicious," she said. "Thank you ever so much."

Mrs. Harper fussed over her until Pauline was seated at the kitchen table, a glass of cold milk accompanying the still-warm bread. As Pauline sank her teeth into the first bite, realization struck her.

"James!"

He hung up the phone, having finished his call to headquarters, and came into the kitchen. "What? What's wrong?"

Pauline chewed and swallowed, eyes wide. Mrs. Harper hovered by the sink, eagerly waiting to hear what she had to say. Discretion sank in belatedly. "Er, nothing, sorry," she said, loathing the lie as it left her lips.

James's eyes flickered between her and Mrs. Harper, and he nodded. "Not to worry," he said casually.

Neither said anything more until Pauline had finished her snack, sincerely thanked her landlady, and that good woman had reluctantly left the apartment once more, this time for good.

Pauline wasted no more time. "James, Miss Lewis couldn't have been killed last night."

"What? What do you mean? Why not?"

"When you opened the back door of her house this morning, I smelled freshly baked bread. In the shock of hearing the news, I didn't pay any attention, and I'd forgotten until just now, when Mrs. Harper brought me a slice of her bread. Miss Lewis has to have been killed this morning, after she'd already taken the bread out of the oven."

James's jaw dropped. "How could I have missed that?"

"Because you are not a housewife," Pauline said. She wasn't, either, but she at least had more experience with housewifery than a man like James did.

"Then it couldn't have been the nephew," James said slowly. "Though we still should call on him to see if he has any insights into his aunt's death. Miss Lewis was alive and well when he left."

"She was in her clothing because she'd already dressed for the day, not because she hadn't gone to bed," Pauline said.

"The doctor should be able to confirm that, but thank you, Pauline, you've saved us going in the wrong direction before getting his report. We'll need to get back to Mrs. MacNeill and ask if she saw or heard anyone there this morning, before the milkman arrived."

A chill settled in the pit of Pauline's stomach. "I doubt it. She would have said something to me if she had. She was talkative enough about the milkman's arrival, and then you and Officer Wallace showing up, and then me."

"Then either someone managed to sneak in without her noticing, which is unlikely, or..."

Pauline finished his sentence. "Or Mrs. MacNeill had something to do with the murder."

They stared at each other in wordless horror.

"And here I thought she was a typical nosy neighbor," James said. "She wanted to know if we were on to her, that's all."

Pauline's brain caught up with their speculation. "Wait, though—she couldn't have burgled this apartment. She was home all morning. I can attest to that, as I was with her."

James nodded. "True, but then, is it likely that she would have been the murderer herself? Far more likely that she has an accomplice who is performing the actual deeds."

"Or she is the accomplice," Pauline said, still having a difficult time accepting that utterly ordinary woman as a master criminal. "But why?"

"Why would anyone care about Miss Lewis's memoirs, enough to kill?" James said. "It made sense when it was the nephew wanting his inheritance early, or at least felt more plausible. But we add in the robbery here, and it's all a muddle again. I don't suppose she did tell you anything worth killing over? No secret treasure hidden somewhere, no deep dark secrets, no horrible scandals?"

Pauline shook her head. "No, nothing like that. If she did know anything of that sort, she took the information to the grave with her."

James scratched his head. "Then how the deuce are we ever going to find the motive?" He sighed and answered his own question. "I guess this is going to be one of those cases where the motive doesn't matter, what matters is the physical evidence. And if we prove that the murderer had to have been at Miss Lewis's house this morning, and that he or she couldn't have been there without Mrs. MacNeill being aware of it, and if she continues to insist she saw nothing and no one, we will have no choice but to arrest her, whether we can come up with a reasonable motive or not."

"We should—or I suppose you should—find out if Mrs. MacNeill has a connection to anyone in Miss Lewis's past." Pauline did not need her notes to remember the names of the individuals Miss Lewis had spoken so fondly of over the past few weeks. "Her fiancé, Tom Martens, died in '81, but he might have some family still living in the area. Or the person who bought the Martens farm after he died might know more. There is a chance her nephew might still be involved, Samuel Crane is his name, her sister's son. Any of her former colleagues might know something. Then there's her former students, any one of them might know something more about her past than what she revealed to me."

James was scribbling all this down. He grimaced at her last suggestion. "She taught half the town over the years, we'd never be able to interview all of them. As it is, there's enough here to keep Wallace busy for a month," he said. "The chief won't like this being dragged out that long."

"Then let me interview some of them," Pauline said.

"Now look here—" James began.

"I can tell them it's to complete her memoirs in her honor," Pauline said. "It's the perfect excuse. I can meet with them in public, so I won't be in danger, and you can even have

Officer Wallace or someone else watching me, to make sure I'm safe. It might be the best way to find a connection."

"You want me to use you as bait," James said flatly.

Pauline pushed away from the table and motioned to the mess that was her living room. "Look at this, James! They came into my home and did this! Now you don't even want me to sleep here until they are caught. Yes, I want you to use me as bait. Anything to bring these villains to justice as soon as possible, for Miss Lewis's sake as well as my own."

James walked to the window and looked out. "The chief is here, and Wallace with your bicycle. I'll ask the chief what he thinks, but you must promise me to abide by his decision. If he says no, I don't want you running off into danger on your own to pursue this yourself, no matter how angry you are."

Pauline was angry, but not so much that she had lost all sense. This person had already killed once; she had no desire to follow Miss Lewis into oblivion.

"Very well," she conceded.

If Chief Gordon didn't agree, she would have to come up with another plan that he would agree to. This situation could not be allowed to continue. The murderer must be found and apprehended.

She would accept nothing less.

CHAPTER SIX
Moving Forward

The wheels of bureaucracy began to turn, and Pauline found herself on the outside of the affair looking in, though she was in her own home. Chief Gordon wasn't interested in anything she had to say until he had heard it all from James first, nor was she permitted to participate in sorting through any more of the debris scattered throughout the apartment. Her heart sank when she saw Officer Wallace pick up one of her typed pages and glance over it first quickly, then slowly and with more interest as he began to read.

"Say, this is pretty good stuff," he said. "Where's the rest of it?"

Luckily for Pauline's over-strained nerves, James noticed what Wallace was doing and left his report to berate the youngster.

"Never mind that!" he said, taking the paper from the unfortunate young man, who wilted under James's disapproving scowl. "We are not here to snoop through Miss Gray or Miss Jones's belongings, only to look for any clues the thief might have left behind, or any notes from Miss Lewis. Keep your mind on business, not other people's affairs!"

"Sorry," Wallace muttered, his flaming cheeks clashing with his hair.

Despite this intervention, Pauline had a horrible sinking feeling that her secret was out. No matter how discreet the policemen were, once one extra person knew a secret, the information began to spread, and soon everyone would know. Her days of hiding Emma Daring behind a cloak of anonymity were over.

It was almost too much to take in on top of everything else.

One thing for which she could be thankful was that Sarah's possessions remained almost untouched. It appeared the burglar had given her room a cursory search, then left it alone to focus on Pauline's belongings.

"How did he know the difference?" Wallace wondered aloud.

"The nurse's uniforms hanging in Miss Jones's wardrobe would be a good clue," James answered dryly.

It was a good question. However panicked the burglar might have been, he or she was still observant enough to tell the difference between the two women's clothing and belongings, and reasoned enough to not destroy Sarah's things needlessly. It added another layer to the picture Pauline was building of the killer: this was a person who was careful enough to only search where it seemed necessary, yet desperate enough to murder.

Unfortunately, that still wasn't enough for her to put a face or a name to the individual, nor did it do much to ease the humiliation of seeing the policemen examining her undergarments, no matter how respectful they were. It was a relief when the officers finished their search and left with vague promises to keep her informed.

Chief Gordon hadn't committed himself to anything regarding Pauline's suggestion of questioning Miss Lewis's former colleagues and students, stating merely they would have to question Mrs. MacNeill again as well as interview Samuel Crane, Miss Lewis's nephew, before they took any further steps. James reminded Pauline to phone him when she was ready to leave, and then there was nothing but the clatter of boot heels going down the outside steps, and finally, blessed stillness inside the still-disheveled apartment.

Pauline released a long, slow breath, and sank down at the kitchen table, head buried in her hands. It was all too much. Was it really only this morning she had set out so blithely along the road to Miss Lewis's house? It seemed a lifetime ago.

Oh, how her mother would triumph over this. After all of Pauline's insistence on Canton as a calmer, quieter, safer place to live than Albany, now not only to have stumbled into yet another murder investigation, but also to have suffered the indignity of a break-in at her own home! Well, Pauline would not give Mother the satisfaction of crowing over her; she promptly resolved to never tell anyone in her family about this unless she had to.

And for all this to happen while Sarah was away...! Pauline would have to tell her, of course, and what news for her to return home to at the end of the week.

Miss Lewis was *dead*, that kind, gracious woman. Approaching the final years of her life anyway, who could have felt the need to hurry her along into the grave? It was all, all wrong.

On top of everything else, Pauline's identity would soon be revealed to all the world as the author of the Emma Daring novels. How her former classmates would groan or gloat, depending on their disposition, over how far Pauline Gray's lofty ideals had sunk! How her professors would purse their lips in disapproval, that she would waste her talents so. How her neighbors would look at her with scorn, writing trash—harmless trash, but trash nonetheless—to fill her purse.

Pauline remained slumped in her position of despair a few moments longer. Then she lifted her head and set her lips firmly.

No matter. No matter what anyone said or thought, she was done moaning over it. Life was too precious to spend it fretting over things she couldn't change. If there was anything good that had come out of her encounters with murder, it was that realization.

She got up from the table filled with fresh resolve. She would clean this apartment from top to bottom, then go on out to Ruby and James's house, and one way or another, she would find a way to bring justice for herself and Sarah as well as for Miss Lewis.

One step at a time.

The cleaning went better than Pauline could have imagined, thanks solely to Mrs. Harper returning as soon as she heard the thump-thump of Pauline opening the storage closet and pulling out the mop and bucket. That good lady insisted on helping, and did much of the hard labor herself while Pauline smoothed crumpled book pages and organized her papers.

"I doubt we'll ever get the ink stain out of the hearthrug, though," Mrs. Harper said, glowering at the offending blot.

Pauline blushed, hoping Mrs. Harper wouldn't notice that the stain was a few weeks old and therefore couldn't have been caused by the thief.

"And I'd like to put fresh sheets on the beds, but I can't find any spare linens," Mrs. Harper continued.

"Oh, Mr. Berger collected the sheets yesterday," Pauline explained. "He always picks them up on Wednesday and returns them on Friday. But it doesn't matter so much, as I won't be sleeping here tonight, and Sarah won't return until late Saturday."

"Gracious, it will be an uncomfortable homecoming for Miss Jones unless the police have caught the villain before then," Mrs. Harper commented.

It would indeed. That gave Pauline a deadline. Two days—two and a half including the rest of this day—to find and stop a murderer. Could she do it? She would have to.

"Mrs. Harper, did you know Miss Lewis at all?"

"Gracious, dearie, everyone knew her. She must have taught half the town in her time." Mrs. Harper shook her head sadly as her strong hands wrung out the cleaning cloth. "I don't think I've quite taken in the fact that she's passed, poor soul, I've been that upset by what's happened here. I suppose you can't tell me anything more about it than what Lieutenant Richardson did?"

Pauline sat back on her heels, having recovered the very last piece of paper from her desk, hidden under the old wingback chair she and Sarah always offered to James when he stopped by for a visit. "I really can't. He trusts me to be discreet, you know."

"Well, I wouldn't want to encourage you to break that trust, then. It is such a shame, that good woman. I can't imagine who would want to harm her, any more than I can think of someone wanting to break in here. It must be a madman, don't you think?"

Pauline disagreed—there was a chilling sanity to these events, a pattern that didn't make sense to her but surely did to the murderer. Still, she didn't have the energy to contradict Mrs. Harper. "Mmm," she said noncommittally, smoothing the crumpled paper. "I don't suppose there's anything or anyone you can think of from your schooldays who might have held a grudge against her?" She recalled back to the conversation at the sewing bee. "A parent who didn't approve of her teaching methods, or a child who resented her?"

"Nothing like that, goodness me. We all adored her. She was the kindest teacher any of us had! Strict, but we all knew we could trust her with absolutely anything."

Pauline's shoulders sagged. She had known it was a forlorn hope—and she hadn't yet received official permission to investigate at all—but it would have made things so much easier if

Mrs. Harper had known right away of someone who had let a grudge fester for years and years until it spilled over into violence, and then tried to hide any evidence pointing to his guilt by making sure Miss Lewis hadn't already told Pauline about him.

A new idea slowly uncurled in her mind. "Mrs. Harper—you said everyone trusted her. You mean that people would have told her their secrets?"

"I never did, but I suppose some probably did. Girls who didn't have friends or parents to talk to found her a safe listener to all their woes, boys who had ambitions everyone else laughed at, that sort of thing."

It all came back to secrets. Something Miss Lewis knew that someone didn't want revealed—and would kill to protect.

Pauline knew whom she had to speak to next, regardless of what James expected of her. The police chief hadn't forbidden her to interfere; she wasn't breaking her promise to abide by his decision if he hadn't made that decision yet.

"Everything looks wonderful, Mrs. Harper," she said, rising to her feet. "Better than it did before. I can't thank you enough."

Her landlady waved off her thanks. "Get along with you. If we can't help each other out once in a while, where does that leave us?" she said. "Are you sure you are up to riding that bicycle all the way to Richardsons, dearie?"

Pauline smiled as she set the lone piece of paper on her desk. "I'll be fine, but thank you. James said he would send someone to accompany me, if not join me himself. Are you going to be all right here by yourself?" she asked, struck by the sudden concern. She didn't think the intruder would return—but then she hadn't expected an intruder in the first place.

"No need to fret, I'll lock my doors and windows," Mrs. Harper promised as she departed for her own quarters.

Collecting her overnight things did not take Pauline long, nor did telephoning to the station. James was just finishing up with his report, he said. Would Pauline be willing to wait for another fifteen or twenty minutes?

She told him to meet her at the vicarage and rang off before he could object.

Pauline hesitated before stepping through the door. It wasn't fear so much as an irrational conviction that leaving would bring about another disaster. The broken lock still dangled from the door, and would until the locksmith James had promised to send arrived. There was no way to keep anyone out... no way to ensure her privacy would not be violated a second time.

Pauline mentally shook herself. This was utter foolishness. There was no reason for the intruder to return. Mrs. Harper was now fully alert downstairs, and her own privacy couldn't be any more degraded than it already was. The household money and the few items of value she and Sarah owned were safely in her valise until the apartment was safe for them—and Pauline—again.

Leaving the apartment wasn't abandoning her home, though it felt like it. Nor was it cowardice. She was doing what was necessary to protect herself and solve the case.

Her fancies firmly tamped down, Pauline forced herself to close the door and walk down the steps to the street, refusing to even turn her head to look back at the upstairs window as she placed her small bag in the bicycle basket and mounted to ride away. She would not give in to sentimental folly.

Luckily Mrs. Hansen was at home in the white clapboard vicarage beside the Episcopal church. Despite the fact that Pauline had never visited before, the vicar's wife didn't look in the least surprised to see that young woman at her door.

"Miss Gray, how splendid," she said, opening the door wide and ushering Pauline inside. "What can I do for you this afternoon?"

Now that she was here, Pauline's stomach knotted. It hadn't occurred to her that in coming to the Reverend Hansen's wife for information about Miss Lewis's students, she would also have to break the news of Miss Lewis's death. James and Chief Gordon would not be pleased with her for that... but in any case, the reverend ought to know.

"I'm afraid I come with bad news," Pauline said, not coming into the house any further than the shabby but clean front hall. "Have you heard that Miss Lewis was killed this morning?"

Mrs. Hansen took a step back, one hand at her throat. "What? Mercy! No, my dear, I hadn't heard. Oh dear, dear, that is tragic. Poor soul. A pillar of the church, and the community. Oh, we shall miss her." She blinked a few times and then focused in again on Pauline. "Did you say killed, Miss Gray? Not an accident or illness? A heart attack, even?"

Pauline shook her head. "I'm afraid not. I don't think the police want the news spread, but it was murder." She hesitated a moment, then plunged ahead with the rest of the tale. "And my apartment was burgled shortly after, which leads me to suspect it had something to do with Miss Lewis's past. I was hoping you might know of someone who would know what that might be."

Mrs. Hansen stared at her. "I think," she said at last, "you had better come in and tell me all of it."

Half an hour later, Pauline left the vicarage with a list of names and a new warmth in her soul. She hadn't expected to be comforted and calmed by this visit, but Mrs. Hansen's genuine warmth and kindness had gone a considerable way toward thawing the ice that had locked her insides ever since seeing James at Miss Lewis's house that morning.

There was evil and hatred in the world, yes, but kindness and compassion as well. Between Mrs. Harper and Mrs. Hansen, and even James's concern for her, Pauline had ample proof of that.

CHAPTER SEVEN
At the Farm

Supper at the Richardson house that evening was an awkward affair. Ruby was genuinely concerned for Pauline and distressed over the case, but was also firm in her rule that one did not discuss such matters at the table. James had a weary crease between his eyebrows that spoke to a long and troublesome afternoon, and he didn't contribute much to the conversation at all. Pauline felt uncomfortable enough about interposing into their family life, not to mention the exhaustion from the day catching up to her. Were it not for young Jeremy, Ruby's son from her previous marriage, chatting excitedly about baseball and fishing, it would have been a silent meal.

Ruby shooed Pauline out of the kitchen, refusing her offer to help with dishes, as soon as the meal was over. Feeling thoroughly worn out, Pauline escaped to the guest bedroom. James caught up with her right before she entered the small but pleasant room.

"We brought Mrs. MacNeill in for questioning this afternoon," he said. "She swears things happened as she said they did, but it was hard to get much sense out of her once she realized we suspected her. Can't tell if her tears and outrage are protective or genuine." He looked tired.

Pauline felt a pang at not sharing the information she had received from Mrs. Hansen with him, but the less he knew about her plans, the less likely he was to try to forbid her from pursuing them. "I still find it hard to imagine her as a killer, lack of motive aside."

"I know," James said. "But when you look at evidence, it's hard to get away from the fact that she must have seen the killer arrive, so she's either shielding him or lying to protect herself."

Pauline frowned. "I feel as though there's something we're missing, something from the apartment that plays a role in this as well..." She shook her head, frustrated. "It's not coming to me."

"You've had a long day," James said sympathetically. "Get some rest. Maybe it will make more sense in the morning."

Pauline managed a smile. "Good advice. Thank you. Good night."

"Good night."

It was too early for sleep, so Pauline pulled the small stack of books she had packed out of her bag and placed them on the nightstand. Her hands closed more tightly around *Cranford*. If she closed her eyes, she could almost imagine herself back at Miss Lewis's, browsing delightedly through her bookshelves, so pleased to find this old friend, one she'd read many times without it ever growing stale. Pauline opened her eyes. For a moment or two, she didn't think she'd be able to read it—not now, not ever again—but she swallowed past the lump in her throat and lectured herself sternly.

"What sort of a tribute to Miss Lewis would that be?" she asked of herself. "To dishonor her final act of generosity to you! You will read this story, and you will enjoy it, just as you always have, and you will think fondly of Miss Lewis when you close its pages. For shame! Will you let her murderer take this away from you as well?"

Her throat aching and her eyes stinging, Pauline sat down in the cane-bottomed chair by the window, and opened the dull red leather-bound cover of the book. It took her longer than she would have liked to lose herself in the story, but by the time she finally did close the pages, her soul was refreshed.

She still wasn't sure she would be able to sleep, but the moment she crawled between the fresh-smelling sheets and pulled the bright patchwork quilt up to her chin, Pauline's eyes closed and she slept soundly, with no dreams that she could remember, until the sun shining through the curtains woke her the next morning.

She was bewildered at first at the strange curtains, the odd placement of the bed, the voices coming from the other rooms... until memory flooded back, and she knew where she was, and why.

Pauline stifled a groan as she climbed out of the comfortable bed. Would that yesterday had only been a dream! She wasn't sure she had the strength to endure this race to the end. Nothing but her sense of propriety made her able to dress, wash her face, and pin up her hair rather than getting back into bed and pulling the cozy quilt over her face.

Perhaps she ought to let the police handle this one... was it really right for her to insist on participating? Or was it cowardice to want to hide from this?

She probably ought to start with breakfast. No sense trying to see the world from a correct perspective on an empty stomach.

"Oh, Pauline!" Ruby said as her guest entered the kitchen, a hint of reproach in her tone. "I was going to prepare a tray for you."

Pauline smiled and took the heavy tea kettle from her friend. "I should be the one waiting on you, Ruby, not the other way around."

Ruby rolled her eyes. "Oh, you sound just like James. I am fit as a fiddle, I do not need any fussing over!"

Pauline couldn't help but laugh even as she worked the pump at the sink to fill the kettle. "Fair enough. I will not coddle you if you do not coddle me."

Ruby's lips curved as she took the filled kettle back and set it on the woodstove. "Agreed." She placed a hand on the small of her back and stretched out the kinks. "James has promised me indoor plumbing just as soon as we can manage it. It won't come a moment too soon for me."

"Your kitchen may be old-fashioned, but it is charming," Pauline said, looking around the light-filled room.

Ruby made a face. "You wouldn't say that if you had to cook and clean in here! Besides," leaning close, "indoor plumbing means *running hot water* for baths and no more outhouse."

Pauline couldn't argue against the appeal of that.

After a light breakfast of fresh biscuits and Ruby's homemade wild strawberry jam, Pauline left the Richardson house with the excuse of wanting to check on the apartment. It wasn't only an excuse—she did want to see how the place had fared overnight, and collect one or two items she had forgotten the previous day—but it was not her only reason for going out. She had her list of people to speak to about Miss Lewis's past, and she was determined to get to as many of them as possible before Chief Gordon remembered to forbid it.

She felt a small amount of guilt over going out unaccompanied, given James's concern for her safety, but she honestly did not think she was in danger. If the murderer was keeping that close a watch on Pauline's movements, they would know that she had already been questioned by the police and told everything she knew. Killing her now would do nothing.

Besides, she had to do *something*. Tempting though it was to leave this particular case to the police, Pauline could not do that. Her conscience wouldn't allow it.

To her relief, nothing about the house on Pleasant Street had changed overnight. Mrs. Harper popped out of her front door as soon as she saw Pauline through the window, and told her nothing had disturbed her sleep in the slightest.

"And Roger Denney from the locksmith is coming by this afternoon to replace the broken lock," she added. "I'll give you a copy of the new key as soon as it's available."

That bit of business taken care of, Pauline set off in search of what once was the Martens farm and now belonged to the Ingersoll family. Mrs. Ingersoll's name was on the list given to Pauline by Mrs. Hansen, and given that they had already met at the sewing bee, she seemed a natural choice for Pauline to question first.

Their farm was outside the village limits, partway up the long, steep slope of Waterman Hill. Pauline was thankful to dismount when she reached the split rail fence surrounding their front yard. It was a snug, tidy little farm, with a white house, red barn, and blue silo. Next door was a smaller farm, and the Berger house was across the road. All in all, a pleasant corner of the community. As she stepped onto the pathway leading to the house she saw Mrs. Ingersoll and Mrs. Addison coming around from the backyard carrying an empty laundry basket between them, the wash waving merrily on the line behind their backs.

Mrs. Ingersoll recognized her and waved, setting the basket on the grass and coming forward to greet her guest.

"Good morning, Miss Gray! I thought I might see you soon. Mrs. Hansen telephoned me yesterday and told me about poor Miss Lewis, and said that you wanted to finish her memoirs in her honor and would I be able to help."

Pauline was dazzled at having her path thus smoothed for her. "Yes," she said, meaning every word. "I feel it is the least I can do. Miss Lewis didn't want her loved ones to be forgotten after her passing, and I find I can't bear to think of her being forgotten either, not if I can help it."

"Well, that isn't too likely," said Mrs. Ingersoll. "Not when so many of us have her to thank for our ability to read, write, and figure! But I think it's a splendid thing you're doing for her memory, and I'm proud to help in any way I can."

"Such a dreadful thing," Mrs. Addison agreed, her face pale and somber. "It must have been someone from the County Home, don't you think? They probably tried to break into her house to steal the silver, except she caught them in the act and they turned violent." She shuddered. "I could never bear to live so close to the poorhouse. I'd go in fear of my life and my children's lives every day!"

"Well now, I suppose they can't help being poor," Mrs. Ingersoll said tolerantly. "And I must say Miss Lewis never gave them any reason to want to harm her. Always ready to employ one of them to tend her garden, or mend her fence, or do little jobs around the house. Doesn't seem likely they'd turn on her."

Mrs. Addison shook her head. "Father always said to never trust anyone who ended up in the poorhouse, that they were there for a reason. Miss Lewis should have known better than to encourage them! She even went so far as to allow that Kilpatrick girl to stay with her after her father threw her out of the house for her shame! Said no baby should be born in the poorhouse, no matter what his parents had done. And now look at where it got her."

"I wouldn't have wanted the lass in my house, to be sure," Mrs. Ingersoll agreed. "But there, I have my boys to worry about. Miss Lewis had only herself. I don't think her kindness toward Lucy Kilpatrick and her poor wee son is what caused her death."

Mrs. Addison pinched her lips together, nodded curtly to Pauline, and crossed the yard to her own house. Mrs. Ingersoll watched her go with a faintly superior smile on her face. "Poor

Cathy, she always was a mite too narrow-minded for her own good. Well, Miss Gray! I suppose you want to look around the place, see where Miss Lewis would have lived if Tom Martens hadn't died? Poor soul. Well, well, they're together again now."

"Miss Lewis said there was an accident here on the farm, but she didn't give me any more details than that—she didn't want to talk about it," Pauline said. "How did he die?"

It had occurred to her that perhaps Tom had been murdered, and Miss Lewis killed now in order to cover up the past dreadful crime.

Mrs. Ingersoll shattered that suspicion with her response. "Oh, I don't blame her for not wanting to talk about it, even after all these years. I had nightmares after I first learned about it when Hank brought me here to live. Just dreadful. He was out cutting hay, and the scythe slipped..." She must have seen Pauline's face turn slowly green, for she cut short the rest of the details. "Blood poisoning," she finished abruptly.

That certainly did not sound like murder, but no wonder Miss Lewis didn't care to think back to it. Even if Pauline had been interested in marriage, she wouldn't have wanted to marry a farmer. For one, she didn't think she was suited to life as a farmer's wife. For another, she doubted she had the endurance to bear up under the dangers and suffering such a life entailed. Too many things could go wrong with farming.

"But here," continued Mrs. Ingersoll, picking up the empty laundry basket again and moving toward the back door. "After Mrs. Hansen telephoned, I looked out some old letters that had been stashed away in a closet when Hank's father bought the place, and found a couple from Miss Lewis to Tom. They're on the kitchen table, so long as those imps of mine and the Addison youngsters haven't torn them to pieces." She shook her head. "I'm always so glad when school ends for the year, and within a week I'm wishing it would start again! Lucky for me the Addisons live so close, our young'uns can run around together and wear each other out. I keep them here when Mrs. Addison runs errands, and she does the same for me."

"That is fortunate," Pauline said absently, still trying to distract her mind from the image of Tom Martens swinging a scythe and—

"Ah, here they are!" said Mrs. Ingersoll, stepping into the kitchen. "Right, you lot, out you go. And mind you stay out of my clean linens!" she called as a whirlwind of small boys blew past Pauline to race down to the small brook that flowed out past the clothesline.

"I ought not to complain," she said, handing the yellowed envelopes to Pauline. "Mrs. Addison took them for me yesterday so I could go to town and do the marketing for the week. Well, there you are, my dear. I wish I had thought to look in that closet before, I would have liked to give them to Miss Lewis herself. At least it will help them both be remembered now."

While Pauline cautiously eased the fragile letters out of their envelopes, a light tap came on the kitchen door, followed immediately by a stout woman entering the house.

"Ach, Mrs. Ingersoll, how many times have I told you to let me wash your sheets for you!" exclaimed Margret Berger. "We are only across the road, and it would be my pleasure after all the help you and Mr. Ingersoll have given Heinrich and me when we first moved here."

Mrs. Ingersoll laughed. "I know, Mrs. Berger, but I can't seem to break the habit. Besides, you have enough work to do with paying customers, surely."

Mrs. Berger shook her head severely, then turned to greet Pauline. "Good morning, Miss Gray. We don't often see you out this way."

"No, although the countryside is so pleasant out here I think I must start cycling this way more often," Pauline said. "I had a lovely conversation with your sister the other day, at the sewing bee for Ruby Richardson."

"Yes, we missed you there, Mrs. Berger," Mrs. Ingersoll broke in.

Mrs. Berger spread work-roughened hands. "Too much work! I am glad Klara went, though. She gets—oh, I do not know the word. Loses interest in things to do."

"Bored?" Pauline suggested diffidently.

"Ah, that is it. Fifteen years in this country and still there are words that slip away from me!" Mrs. Berger said, shaking her head.

"I couldn't learn German if my life depended on it," said Mrs. Ingersoll. "You forget maybe one word every six months, and have barely the hint of an accent. I don't think you need despair! Oh—" looking out the window. "There go my sheets! You boys!"

The guilty parties took one look at the wrathful figure descending on them from the house and scampered away, leaving the mud-streaked sheets tangled on the ground where they had fallen.

"Those rascals!" growled Mrs. Berger, coming out with Pauline behind Mrs. Ingersoll. "They played the nasty trick on my

Heinrich yesterday. Mrs. Addison was supposed to be watching them, but ach, she lets them do whatever they please. Oh, Mrs. Ingersoll, now you *must* let me wash them for you!"

Mrs. Ingersoll smiled and sighed and bundled the once-crisp sheets up to pass along to the German woman. "I suppose I must. Thank you, Mrs. Berger. Miss Gray, I'm sorry our chat has been interrupted. Shall we try again? Miss Gray is trying to finish up Miss Lewis's memoirs, as a tribute of sorts," she explained to Mrs. Berger.

"That is good!" exclaimed Mrs. Berger. "She was a gracious lady. She always offered Heinrich a cup of tea when he dropped off the laundry for her, and always asked if we had heard recently from our boy back in the old country. We shall miss her."

And that, Pauline thought ruefully, seemed to be the way everyone felt. How to find who had killed Miss Lewis when everyone who knew her respected and liked her so much? Even those who disapproved of all her kindness, such as Mrs. Addison, couldn't say anything truly bad about her.

The rest of the conversation did not provide any additional insight, though Mrs. Ingersoll did insist that Pauline take the letters with her. It didn't seem likely that they would contain a clue, being merely notes from a young lady to her sweetheart about their future plans, but one never knew. Perhaps a closer study of their contents would help.

Two boys stood by Pauline's bicycle when she returned to it, and she gave them both suspicious looks.

"No tricks here, I hope," she said severely.

The taller of the two laughed. "No, ma'am. We don't do things like that anymore. Besides, it isn't nice to play jokes on a stranger."

"Only on people you know?" Pauline asked, amused despite herself.

"You bet!" the smaller boy piped up. "It's more funny then."

The older boy rolled his eyes.

"I heard you were playing tricks on poor Mr. Berger yesterday," Pauline said.

The boys glanced at each other. "I sure wasn't," the older one said. "I had to help Pa. Were you, Charlie?"

The younger shook his head. "Naw. Me and Bobby were out playing in the woods with Pete and Andy and Mikey. It was swell. Normally Mrs. Addison makes us stay where she can see us, but yesterday we just did what we wanted. Went wading in the brook, climbed trees, and everything!" His eyes were round and he waved his hands in the air as he continued. "She *never* lets us play in the brook, 'cause she can't swim and so she's always afraid we'll drown, even though it's not that deep." His nose wrinkled with childish scorn at the folly of adult fears.

Pauline smiled at his enthusiasm even as she felt sympathy for the poor, overworked mothers, trying to keep such energetic boys out of mischief all the time. No wonder Mrs. Ingersoll had been so pleased by her chance to get away for a short while! Even marketing would seem restful in comparison.

Shaking her head in wonder, she mounted her bicycle and rode on to the next place on her list.

CHAPTER EIGHT
More Suspects

The next person Pauline wanted to question was Samuel Crane, Miss Lewis's nephew. She was sure the police had already done so, but the questions they would have asked him were not necessarily the same ones she wanted to ask. She was quite certain neither James nor Chief Gordon would approve of this course of action. Fortunately, she had an excuse at hand to look Mr. Crane up and offer him her condolences.

As she had suspected, Mr. Crane was at Miss Lewis's house, inventorying the contents and making copious notes. He seemed startled at first when Pauline knocked on the door, but upon her introduction of herself as the person working with Miss Lewis on her memoirs, his face smoothed into a smile.

"Of course, the newspaper woman," he said. "Aunt Anita told me about you. Please, come in. I'm afraid everything is at sixes and sevens. The police just finished up here this morning, and asked me to check to see what, if anything, is missing. What a task, with all Aunt Anita's knickknacks! Still, I might be able to rustle up a cup of coffee."

Pauline had never considered herself a particularly dense individual, but it only now occurred to her, standing on the back doorstep, that if Mr. Crane *was* the murderer and vandal, she was offering him the perfect opportunity to do away with her as well. And she had been so smugly certain that she would be safe in her investigations!

She resisted the urge to take a step back. Surely the worst thing she could do would be to show fear at this point! If he was not the murderer, he would be mortally offended, and if he was the murderer, he would take her fear as a sign of weakness and act accordingly. No, she had been foolish enough to put herself in this position, the only thing to do now was to brazen it out. But oh, wouldn't James scold when he found out!

Pauline cleared her throat. "Would you consider me terribly rude if I preferred to remain outside? You see, it's so soon after—after your aunt's passing. I'm not sure I could bring myself to go in—in where it happened."

A flash of something—was it irritation?—crossed Mr. Crane's face, only to be quickly replaced by his former bland smile. "Of course, of course." He closed the door behind him and motioned around to the side of the house, where a whitewashed wrought iron bench sat amidst the roses.

Pauline seated herself in the middle of the bench, leaving no room for Mr. Crane to join her. His mouth turned down at the corners at that, but once again he said nothing. He leaned against a young cherry tree, the delicate white blossoms of spring replaced now by green fruit waiting to ripen, and waited for her to speak.

"I wished to pass my condolences to you, Mr. Crane, on the loss of your aunt," Pauline began. "I had only known her a short time, but from the stories she told I could see what a rich life she led. Her death will be felt by the entire community." To her horror, her voice thickened on the last words and real tears sprang to her eyes. This was hardly appropriate detective work!

Still, the truth in her words could not be denied, nor would she choose to denigrate Miss Lewis's memory by spouting false platitudes, even if it was to catch her killer.

"That's mighty kind of you, Miss Gray," Mr. Crane said, though he did not go so far as to offer her a handkerchief. "I can't say it's really sunk in yet. Even as I'm sorting through all Aunt Anita's things, I keep expecting her to come around the corner and tell me to stop fussing with it all." He stopped, staring into space. "No, it just doesn't seem real."

Pauline luckily had her own handkerchief in her bag, and was able to dab at her eyes until they stopped watering. "It must be a comfort to you, to be in the house she loved so well."

He crossed his arms in front of his chest. "I suppose. I can't live here, though. My work is in Lisbon, and I can't be trying to get between the two places every day. I guess I'll have to sell it, much as I hate to." He didn't sound very sad about it; in fact, his eyes gleamed as he spoke.

It was not evidence, nor even a sign of bad character—plenty of people these days would be thankful for the chance to put a little extra money in their pocket—but Pauline resented his attitude all the same. How dare he so casually speak of selling Miss Lewis's haven? It was almost sacrilegious.

"Oh? What do you do for work?" she asked, attempting to sound merely politely curious.

"I'm foreman at the plant," he said. At her puzzled expression, he clarified, "The powdered milk plant."

"Ah, yes," Pauline said. Her journalistic instincts got the upper hand, and she said, "That sounds like something my readers would find interesting. I wonder if I might have a tour someday, and an interview?"

She hadn't meant her inquiry to be a sop to the man's vanity, but it worked as one. Before her very eyes he puffed up, seemingly growing taller, and he beamed all over his broad, reddish face. "That's awfully good of you!" he said. "I'd be tickled pink. And speaking of your writing, Miss Gray, I'd like to tell you my aunt was some pleased at working with you on her little project. No doubt the story of an old woman's life was tedious to a journalist like yourself, but it sure did brighten her days."

"Thank you, but I didn't find it tedious at all!" Pauline cried. "Your aunt's life may have been simple, but it was full and rich. In fact, I intend to carry on with her memoirs, as a tribute to her memory. With your permission, of course," she added belatedly.

He blinked his large, pale eyes repeatedly. "Oh," he said. "Er. Well. I suppose... that is, yes, of course. Why not?"

This was all very well and good, but it didn't seem to be getting them any further. Pauline twiddled with the corner of her handkerchief and wondered what to say next. She cast about in her mind, and remembered something just in time to keep the silence from growing too awkward.

"I also wanted to apologize," she said.

"Apologize, Miss Gray?"

"Yes, your aunt had lent me some books, you see, and before I had a chance to return them, someone broke into my apartment, and I'm afraid they took some damage. Pages bent, the spines weakened, that sort of thing. I am certain someone at the university would be able to repair them, but it may take some time." She watched him narrowly, but his face showed no expression save concern when she spoke of the break-in.

"That's terrible! I hope the thieves didn't take anything of value. Don't you worry about those books another moment, Miss Gray. You've got enough on your mind. In fact, why don't you keep them? I'm sure my aunt would like you to have them. I don't have much time for reading, myself."

Pauline managed to repress her wince. "That's kind of you," she said. "Thank you."

There didn't seem to be anything left to say. Pauline rose to her feet and held out one gloved hand. "Thank you for your time, Mr. Crane, and I'm sorry to take you away from your duties here."

"Not at all," he replied, giving her hand a brief shake and then dropping it immediately. "Thank you for coming. Er... you won't forget about that tour?"

Pauline assured him she would not, and made her way back out through the garden and to the sidewalk where she had left her bicycle. She couldn't help but look mournfully at the little white house with the green roof and shutters as she mounted the machine. The next time she saw it, it would likely have new owners, people who cared nothing for the library or the andiron owls or English tea in thin china cups.

It simply wasn't right. But what could she do?

"Miss Gray!"

Pauline turned her head in the direction of the call. A man a few years older than herself stood in front of Mrs. MacNeill's brick house, waving at her. Pauline hesitated. Who was this and why was he calling her?

The man came closer. "You are Miss Gray, aren't you? My mother saw you out the window and said that's who you are."

"I am," Pauline admitted. "Might I inquire who you are?"

"Sorry," he said, mopping his face with a crisp white handkerchief. "Angus MacNeill. I live out toward Hermon, but I am staying with my mother until this mess is cleared up."

"I see," Pauline said, for lack of a better response. What did this have to do with her?

"Miss Gray, I realize this is impolite, me accosting you on the street like this, but I need your help. I've heard that you sometimes assist the police with their cases, and since you were friendly with Miss Lewis and were here right after she was killed..." He stopped and wiped his face again. "Sorry," he repeated. "This is awkward. The police seem to think my mother had something to do with Miss Lewis's death, just because they have some supposed evidence that Miss Lewis was killed in the morning and my mother didn't see anyone coming or going from her house at that time. I don't understand it all, but I know my mother had nothing to do with the murder. It's absurd even to think it! Murder and my mother don't belong in the same sentence."

"I'm afraid I still don't see what this has to do with me," Pauline said, though she had a sinking feeling she did know.

"You have to convince the police to leave my mother alone," Mr. MacNeill said. "Please! Talk to Mother again, and see if you can understand why her story doesn't match what the police say had to have happened. I know she's telling the truth, but I can't make the police believe me. If you can make sense of it, they'll listen to you. It's dreadful of me to just come right out and ask you this, when we've never even met, but I don't know what else to do. My mother needs help, and I can't give it to her."

Pauline couldn't help but hear the sincerity in his voice. No matter what else might or might not be true, Mr. MacNeill was honestly worried for his mother.

The question was, could she believe the rest of his claim? James had said that they didn't think Mrs. MacNeill had done the murder herself, rather that she was covering up for someone else. They hadn't any idea who, though. Now here was her son, who was certainly strong enough from his appearance to murder a frail elderly woman, come out of the blue to defend his mother. What if he wasn't here just to defend her, but to protect himself? What if he had done the killing?

But why—why—why? The question beat at Pauline's mind. Nobody seemed to have a motive in this case, save perhaps Samuel Crane, who inherited a house and its contents and would

82

be able to sell both to line his pockets. In these times, it was a strong motive.

Yet despite an instinctive dislike for the man, Pauline wasn't sure she could see him as a murderer. And as the police had determined, if he were the murderer, how could he have gotten into his aunt's house without Mrs. MacNeill noticing? Into and back out again, for that matter. Perhaps the nosy neighbor might have missed either the entrance or the exit, but surely not both.

Then there was the burglary of Pauline's own apartment. How did that fit in? If Mr. Crane was the murderer, it didn't make sense. Nor had he seemed perturbed by the information that she had two of his aunt's books in her possession.

Mrs. MacNeill had to be lying, no matter how much her son insisted she was telling the truth. And if that was the case, than she could have no reason to lie but to protect someone else. Who better to protect than her son? Perhaps his motive lay deep in the past, as Pauline had speculated. What if Miss Lewis had known something about him, something he was desperate to keep hidden?

If that was the case, then his approaching her like this meant that he was not trying to help his mother, but trying to gauge how much Pauline knew about the case, and her life was in danger. Not that he would try to murder her here, in the street, where Mr. Crane could see everything and any passerby was a potential witness. But if she had thought herself in danger by going into Miss Lewis's house, how much more so into the MacNeill house.

On the other hand, if there was an honest mistake somewhere, and Mrs. MacNeill and her son were both innocent of any wrongdoing, could Pauline live with herself for having turned away from the plea for help?

She wrenched her mind back to the present, where Mr. MacNeill was waiting for her answer. She made up her mind.

"I will speak with your mother," she said. "But I can't do it here. I am staying with the Richardson family temporarily, and she can come and speak to me there this afternoon."

If she had been hoping for Mr. MacNeill to confirm her suspicions by pressing her to come into the house, she was disappointed. He reached for her hand and pumped it up and down enthusiastically.

"Thank you, Miss Gray! Thank you very much! I'll bring Mother over right after lunch. I can't tell you how grateful I am!"

He rushed back into the house and Pauline at last began cycling back to the Richardson house. Whether she had made a mistake, only time would tell, but she hoped not. One way or another, they *had* to get to the bottom of this case.

CHAPTER NINE
An Apology Made

James did not often get a chance to come home in the middle of the day, and it was just pure bad luck that this one day, of all days, he was seated at the dining room table waiting to enjoy a hot dinner when Pauline returned to the house. She stopped short, her cheeks flushing with guilt.

"Oh Ruby, I am so sorry," she exclaimed, pressing her hands to her cheeks. "I'm so accustomed to having a light luncheon, it didn't even occur to me that you would make dinner. I should have returned sooner, or at least let you know I would be out. It was so terribly rude of me!"

"Don't fret," Ruby said cheerfully. "We only just sat down. I was going to serve James and Jeremy and wait for you, but as you're here now, we can all eat together."

Pauline removed her hat and gloves, washed her hands, and sat down, wondering how to break the news to James that not only had she defied his wishes by continuing to investigate the case, she had also invited a possible murderer to his house this afternoon. What on earth had possessed her? She picked away at the roast and potatoes until Jeremy spoke up.

"Are you coming down with a fever, Miss Gray? I was just like that with food when I got sick last year. Mother says I've been making up for it ever since." He grinned at her.

"Jeremy," Ruby scolded. "Don't embarrass Miss Gray."

There was nothing for it. Pauline's stomach clenched and her head began to ache, but it was better to speak and get this over with. She set her fork down.

"You're very observant, Jeremy. You'd make a good journalist. I'm not unwell, but I am a little unhappy with myself. Have you ever done something without thinking it through first?"

Jeremy's eyes widened. "Sure! Mother's always telling me to think before I leap. Gosh, you mean grown-ups do that too?"

Pauline glanced at James, whose face had grown suspicious. "Sometimes. And we always feel very foolish afterward."

Jeremy nodded in sympathy. "And then your stomach starts to feel all funny, and you want to tell someone about it but you wish you didn't have to, and you just feel sicker and sicker."

He was astonishingly perceptive for a boy his age. "Exactly."

James cleared his throat. "Jeremy, why don't you run along outside so Miss Gray can talk to your mother and me about what it was she did without thinking?"

Jeremy stood without complaint, even though he hadn't yet had his dessert, and left the table. "No problem, Dad. Don't worry, Miss Gray. Mother and Dad will help you fix whatever your trouble is."

Pauline watched him leave, then turned her gaze to Ruby. "He's a remarkable young man. You should be proud."

Ruby's face creased with pleasure. "I am. Now, tell us what it is that's troubling you. I doubt it's just sorrow over almost making my roast cold."

Pauline drew in as deep a breath as her tight chest would allow, and admitted that she had invited Mrs. MacNeill to come to the house that afternoon.

As she had expected—and, she had to admit, as she richly deserved—James nearly burst from fury.

"Darn it, Pauline! I told you to stay away from this case! I brought you here to be safe, and instead you go ahead and endanger my wife and son as well as yourself! I know you pride yourself on being an independent woman, but this is too much. You have to think of others once in a while instead of only yourself!"

That sounded too much like something her mother might say. Pauline's own temper flared up. "Yes, I made a mistake," she flashed back. "And I am sorry for it. But I *am* thinking of others! I am thinking of Miss Lewis, and of the innocent people who will suffer from being under suspicion if we don't catch the real murderer. I wish I could close my eyes to the situation, but I can't, I simply cannot sit by and do nothing when there is still something I *can* do."

James's eyes were flat and hard. "That still doesn't justify putting Ruby and Jeremy at risk."

Pauline's self-righteous wrath left her in an instant. He was correct. What an arrogant fool she had been! What had she been thinking? She could have asked Mrs. MacNeill to meet her at any public spot, rather than here where there were other innocent people who could be harmed. Her ears buzzed and her breath started coming in gasps.

Ruby coughed.

It was a gentle sound, but it pulled Pauline out of her downward spiral and caused James's gaze to fly to his wife's face. Her expression was unreadable.

"Goodness," she said. "What a tempest in a teapot."

Confusion flashed across James's open face. "What—?"

Ruby continued gently. "You do fuss so, James. Do you honestly think Mr. MacNeill, even if he is a murderer, which I doubt, is going to try to murder three people, two of whom are connected to a police officer investigating this case, as an attempt to hide his guilt in a previous murder? All while his mother stands there and watches? Nonsense!"

"But—" James began.

"Personally, I think Pauline was quite sensible in inviting them here. But as you are so worried, Jeremy can go play baseball with his friends, I will enjoy a pleasant walk in solitude, you can stay here as protection for Pauline, she can talk to Mrs. MacNeill, and hopefully her story will move you one step closer to catching the murderer."

James opened and closed his mouth a few times without sound. Pauline's tense muscles began to ease, and the buzzing in her ears receded. She didn't deserve such graciousness, but she wouldn't compound her error now by protesting that Ruby ought not to be so forgiving. She managed a tight nod.

"Thank you," she said.

James sighed. "Seems you have it all planned out. Who am I to argue?"

Ruby smiled serenely, with a flash of mischief lurking in her eyes. "And, since Jeremy and I ought to leave now to make sure we are both well out of danger's path, that means the two of you will have to clear the table and wash the dishes."

She set her napkin down next to her plate and sailed out of the room triumphantly before either of the other two could gather their wits enough to respond.

James recovered first, breaking into a low, rumbling laugh. "I'd say she got the best of that exchange! What a woman I married." He passed a hand over his smooth head and finally looked Pauline in the eye with his usual frankness. "I'm still mad about this," he admitted, "but what's done is done, and I guess we all do things we afterwards wish we hadn't."

Pauline stood up and began collecting plates to take to the kitchen. "Believe it or not, I was trying to be cautious," she admitted. "I was so proud of myself for not going into the MacNeill house or into Miss Lewis's house when her nephew invited me in. It wasn't until I got back here that I realized I had only succeeded in putting other people in danger as well as myself rather than protecting myself."

James had also started gathering dishes, but at that he stopped short. "Miss Lewis's nephew—gosh darn it, Pauline. I think you'd better tell me exactly what you did while you were out this morning."

She outlined her morning's adventures as they covered the leftovers and put them in the icebox, scraped the plates clean, pumped and heated water, and at last set to washing all the dishes. To his credit, James didn't scold Pauline any more for her escapades. Instead he frowned in concentration as he wiped dry each clean dish she handed him from the sink.

"It's still not much," he said. "But the chief and I haven't had much luck, either. As you found, no one but Crane seems to have a motive, but he has an alibi, and even if he didn't, why would the MacNeill woman protect him?" He scowled blankly at the forks as he set them in their proper drawer. "I don't suppose there was anything useful in the letters Mrs. Ingersoll gave you?"

Pauline shook her head, but stopped as a memory visited her. *The letter...*

"James, have you ever heard of a Miss Janet Arden?"

"Nope," he answered. "Who is she?"

"I don't know, but Miss Lewis received a letter from her the last day I was there. It was in a long white envelope. She didn't seem to recognize the name, either. Did you find the letter or the envelope when you searched the house afterward?"

He frowned in concentration, hands stilling on the plate he was drying. "No," he said at last. "I think I would have remembered it. I can double check with the chief, but I'm fairly certain it wasn't there." He resumed wiping. "It doesn't mean much, though. Miss Lewis might have thrown it away herself."

"True," Pauline admitted.

"Still, I'll check in with the police downstate. I don't suppose you noticed the address?"

"I'm afraid not," Pauline had to confess.

"A pity. She could be from anywhere, even another state. No harm in checking, at least. For now, though, it still seems like Mrs. MacNeill is our likeliest lead. I hate to admit it, but maybe it is a good thing you invited her here. She was too flustered and nervous to make any sense when we questioned her. She might feel more comfortable in a home, with another woman."

Something warmed inside Pauline at that, but she couldn't forgive herself quite that easily. She finished with the last knife and turned from the sink to face James as she dried her hands on the rough homespun towel.

"All the same, it was a dreadful thing to have done, and you had every right to be angry with me for potentially endangering Ruby and Jeremy. Sarah has warned me often enough how thoughtless I can be when I am on the trail of something that matters to me, and I see now I should listen better to her. I promise you this: I will never put innocent lives at risk again. Except my own, when I deem it necessary," she couldn't help adding.

James laughed, sighed, shook his head, and put the knife away safely in the wooden block. "I suppose I can live with that. As long as you don't object to me scolding you when that happens. You may be willing to put your life at risk, but your friends aren't as comfortable with the idea."

On that note, a truck rattled into the driveway and stopped, and Angus MacNeill stepped out of the driver's side to open the door for his mother. James's brows pulled together again in a scowl.

"I thought it was just the mother coming!"

"I told you her son was bringing her," Pauline replied. " I doubt she can drive. Besides, this is why you are here, isn't it?"

"I suppose," he grumbled, but he managed to be polite as he opened the door to the two on the step. Mrs. MacNeill seemed inclined to be frightened of the large policeman in his shirt sleeves welcoming them into his house, and Pauline quickly stepped into the breach.

"It's such a lovely day, why don't we sit here on the porch, Mrs. MacNeill? You and I can have a nice chat, and Lieutenant Richardson and Mr. MacNeill can..." She trailed off helplessly. What she wanted to say was that they could sit quietly and not interfere with the conversation, but how to say that and still sound polite?

James came to her rescue, his eyes twinkling despite himself. "Let me show you my garden, MacNeill. It's coming along nicely despite the cool spring. Now if I can just keep the dratted groundhog away from all the tender shoots!"

Angus MacNeill allowed himself to be led away, and Pauline and Mrs. MacNeill sat down on the white wicker rockers on the front porch. The older woman's eyes kept filling with tears that she would resolutely blink away, and her blue-veined hands trembled. Despite her suspicions, Pauline's heart went out to the woman.

"Miss Gray," she said, "can you tell me why the police are so sure I must have some involvement in this awful thing? I thought the world of Miss Lewis—everyone did—I would never want to cause her harm. The chief said something about me not reporting seeing the murderer, but I don't understand. I didn't see anyone, so how could I report what I didn't see?"

Pauline settled on the straightforward truth. In Mrs. MacNeill's voice, she heard the ring of honest bewilderment and grief. As unlikely as her story was, Pauline believed she had to be innocent.

"You see, Mrs. MacNeill, the evidence shows that Miss Lewis was—was killed early that morning, not late the night before, as the police had originally thought. As your house has such a prominent view of hers, it seems impossible that the murderer could have come there without you seeing him that morning."

Mrs. MacNeill shook her head. "No, there was no one! Unless someone walked across the field from the County Home and snuck in through the back. I might not have noticed a single walker coming from that direction. But anyone coming from town, I must have seen."

Pauline wished briefly it were that easy, but all the objections she and James had had initially to the murderer being someone from the poorhouse still stood, and were in fact stronger now that they knew Miss Lewis had been killed in the early morning rather than at night. A desperate person might try to break into a dark house when its occupants were supposed to be sleeping and try to steal something, but only a fool would do so in daylight.

Miss Lewis being the kind of person that she was, she would probably have given any poor soul some money to help with a new life without him having to resort to a threat in the first place.

"I can't see any of those County Home folk hurting Miss Lewis, though," Mrs. MacNeill continued, unconsciously echoing Pauline's thoughts. "Some people don't trust them, say that they wouldn't be in the home if they hadn't done something bad, but Miss Lewis never believed that. Why, I remember once, a few years ago—" She stopped abruptly. "There, I shouldn't share such things with a young woman of your standing."

"Please," Pauline said. "Anything you can remember about Miss Lewis is helpful. I promise, I won't be shocked."

Mrs. MacNeill seemed doubtful, but continued. "Well, it was a young woman who was—well—she was—she was unmarried, you see, and she was—well—"

"With child?" Pauline supplied. The tips of her ears were hot, but more at Mrs. MacNeill's embarrassment than anything on her own account. She was aware of the facts of life, and she rather suspected she had already heard part of this story from Mrs. Ingersoll and Mrs. Addison.

"Well, yes," Mrs. MacNeill admitted. "Anyway, her dad threw her out of the house, and Miss Lewis took her in so the baby wouldn't have to be born in the poorhouse. There was an awful to-do about it in town. Folk were divided right and left over whether Miss Lewis was encouraging the young woman in her sin or performing an act of Christian charity. Mrs. Hansen was on Miss Lewis's side, wanted the sewing circle to make some baby clothes, but most of the women up and said they would start attending the Presbyterian church if she did any such thing. Old Mr. Baker—he's dead now, dear, you wouldn't have met him—said it was a shame and a disgrace, and that he would write to the bishop. But Miss Lewis didn't give two pins for any of them. She did what she believed to be right and let public opinion go hang."

That sounded like the woman Pauline had come to know over the last few months. "Nothing about this makes sense!" she burst out. "The murder had to have been in the morning because of the bread, but it can't have been in the morning because you didn't see anyone. It looked like a burglary, but nothing was actually taken. Everyone loved Miss Lewis, but someone murdered her." She pressed her hands to her forehead. "Somehow there must be a way to make logic out of this chaos, but I simply cannot see it."

Mrs. MacNeill leaned forward and patted her knee. "There, there, dear. It's good of you to try, but some things are beyond us."

Pauline smiled wanly. She was supposed to be questioning a suspect, not being comforted by one! She cleared her throat and began again.

"Let's start at the beginning of the day, shall we? You were up at what time?"

"Five o'clock," Mrs. MacNeill said promptly. "I like to get a good start to my day, I do. No sense in lazing about half the morning like some people do! Waste all the best hours of the day."

Pauline would have been happy to sleep until nine o'clock every morning, but she hoped Mrs. MacNeill wouldn't notice her guilty blush.

"I finished off the last of the previous day's milk, like I always do, and had a slice of bread and butter for breakfast," Mrs. MacNeill continued, eyes staring into the distance as she remembered. "Then I got my housecleaning out of the way, again, like I always do. The milkman usually comes around eight-thirty—terrible late for new milk, but he has to get to all the folks in the village first, I suppose—and I like to have my work done and out of the way before he arrives. I'd be ashamed to face him with my floors unswept and the dust still on my furniture!"

More and more, Pauline realized she would never make a proper housewife. She rarely even noticed when there was dust on the furniture, and she only swept because she and Sarah had made an agreement to share the chores evenly, and it wouldn't be fair to inflict her work on her friend.

"And you didn't hear or see anything unusual in all that time?" she asked, brushing aside her inadequacy at keeping a proper house.

"No..." Mrs. MacNeill said, but there was doubt in her voice.

Pauline pounced. "There was something!"

Mrs. MacNeill closed her eyes. "Maybe. But it wasn't terribly unusual. I can hear any traffic that might come down this road, you see, even when I can't see it. So few people come out this way that anyone coming is a distraction. But some of them come so regularly that I don't notice them unless they are there out of their usual time."

"And this was something of that sort?"

"It was... let me think. I was shaking out my curtains and—yes, that's right!" She opened her eyes triumphantly. "I wondered if it was about time for them to be laundered again."

Pauline blinked in confusion. What did that signify?

"And I thought it," Mrs. MacNeill continued, "because Mr. Berger was collecting some of Miss Lewis's laundry. I heard his truck, and was surprised he was there so early." She stopped, her eyes rounding. "Why! How on earth did I forget that? Chief Gordon and that lieutenant there asked me over and over again if I'd seen anyone, but I clean forgot about Mr. Berger."

"Because you didn't see him," Pauline murmured automatically, as her mind frantically turned over this new information. "You only heard him. So your mind didn't make that connection."

"That must be it," Mrs. MacNeill agreed. "And then those two got me so frazzled I didn't know if I was on my head or my tail! Well, now. That's good news, isn't it? Mr. Berger must have seen something that will help you. Should I tell Lieutenant Richardson now?"

James and Mr. MacNeill were walking back toward the porch as she spoke, animatedly discussing proper fertilizer for corn and what to do with that new-fangled zucchini Sal Agosti kept urging everyone to plant.

"Yes indeed," Pauline said.

She didn't say anything else until the MacNeills had left, greatly relieved and blithely unaware of the implications of Mrs. MacNeill's restored memory. Then she and James faced each other, differences aside once more.

"You believe her, I take it," James said, not a question.

"I didn't prompt her," Pauline said in response. "I took her back to the start of her day and she remembered it all on her own from there. But James—I saw Mrs. Berger this morning, and she didn't say a word about her husband being at Miss Lewis's on the day of the murder!" Her eyes were wide with dismay, and her hands began to shake. She liked kindly Mr. Berger and his round, practical wife with her ever-twinkling eyes. Even better did she like Mrs. Berger's sister, Klara, with whom she shared a kindred feeling of enjoying spinsterhood. "He can't possibly have had anything to do with this," she said, arguing with herself as much as anyone. "What would his motive be?"

"Right now if we find someone who was in the right place at the right time, I don't care about their motive," James said grimly. "They could be a homicidal maniac for all I care." He scratched his head. "My father fought in the war, you know, and he always said it was a mistake to let the Bergers come here. Maybe he was right."

"James! For shame!" The Bergers were hardly to blame for the war, and in any case, that had been ages ago.

James had the grace to look ashamed. "Well, I dunno. I've always liked Berger, but he could be a rotten 'un after all. In any case, I have to question him."

"Of course." Pauline recognized that. She just wished Mrs. MacNeill had recalled someone else coming by.

Solving mysteries was never as simple and tidy as they seemed on paper. When real people were involved, heartbreak inevitably ensued. For the first time, Pauline wished she'd never gotten involved.

CHAPTER TEN
Unwelcome Confirmation

James left the house immediately afterward to question Mr. Berger. Pauline wandered through the empty rooms and yard for half an hour, trying not to berate herself, before she finally gave up and left for town, making sure to pen a note to Ruby before leaving.

Her feet took her on their accustomed route to her apartment, and Pauline decided she might as well stop by and pick up one or two items she had forgotten to pack the previous day. She only had the pair of gloves she was currently wearing, for one, and they were getting wretchedly dirty, and she wanted fresh stockings as well.

At the house, Pauline was greeted by Al Denney, the postman, just finishing up his rounds for the day.

"Afternoon, Miss Gray," the friendly old man said, tipping his cap. "I was just about to leave your mail with Mrs. Harper, but as you're here now, I can deliver it to you. Any idea how much longer you'll be with James and Ruby? I can start bringing your mail to you there if it's going to be long."

Pauline smiled in gratitude as she took the slim sheaf of letters. A couple of bills, something from her publisher, and an envelope addressed in her mother's distinctive script. Nothing to be ashamed of, but she was just as glad they wouldn't be subjected to Mrs. Harper's scrutiny.

"I hope I shall be returning here very soon," she said. She didn't bother wondering how Mr. Denney knew her current living situation. Not only did news travel fast in a small town, the mailman was usually the one carrying it.

That made her think again about Miss Lewis's letter. If anyone knew the return address, it would be Mr. Denney.

"Mr. Denney, a few days before Miss Lewis was killed, she received a letter from a Janet Arden. You don't happen to remember seeing that letter, do you, and if you do, would you remember the return address?"

"I'm not supposed to talk about post office business with just anyone, Miss Gray," Mr. Denney said, then winked. "But, as I expect you're helping the police solve her murder, just like you did with Bob Ferris, and that business Arabella Warren got mixed up in over in Clayton, you aren't just anybody. And if it helps catch whoever did *that* to Miss Lewis, I'm happy to help." He squinted off into the distance as though looking back through his memories. Pauline help her breath, not wanting to do anything to interfere with his ratiocination.

Mr. Denney slapped his thigh with his cap. "Got it! Don't remember the exact address, but it was from Saratoga Springs."

Pauline let out her breath. It wasn't as much as she had hoped, but at least it would help them narrow the search down.

"Whatever it was, it stirred up Miss Lewis, for certain," Mr. Denney continued. "She had a note all ready to go the next morning when I brought her mail. She wouldn't even put it in the box, handed it to me personally and said it was important it get delivered at once. I put it in my pocket, even, so's I wouldn't lose it in the bag—not that I've ever lost a letter yet, not in my thirty years doing this route, but I wanted to reassure her."

Pauline hardly dared ask this next question, but she had to know. "Do you remember who that note was addressed to?"

"Why, I surely do. I remember because when I got to the Bergers' house I got the letter out, all ready to deliver, and then those Ingersoll and Addison scamps came running out of nowhere and crashed into me, knocking me right over!" Mr. Denney rubbed his back and grimaced. "The eldest Ingersoll lad there at least had the decency to apologize and help me up, but it took ages to get all the mail collected again, and much of it covered in mud and not fit to be seen! I would have given those boys a good hiding if they were mine, but everyone knows Mrs. Addison won't let anyone raise a hand against her boys, and Jim Addison is too soft with her by half to take a firm stand. Those Ingersoll boys aren't half so bad on their own, but put them with the Addison kids and—whew!"

"Yes, but Miss Lewis's letter," Pauline prompted. She didn't much care about poor parenting choices or misbehaving children.

"Yes, Miss, that's what I'm telling you. It was at the Berger house that they knocked it out of my hand."

Mrs. Harper chose that moment to bustle out of the house and join them on the front steps. "I declare, Al Denney, you would get through your mail route twice as fast if you didn't insist on stopping and chatting with every—oh, Miss Gray! I didn't see you there. Have you come back to stay again? The apartment is all ready except the beds. I can't think what is taking Mr. Berger so long with your clean linens."

Pauline's vague dread crystallized in her stomach. "The sheets! Of course!"

Mrs. Harper and Mr. Denney stared at her with near-identical expressions of incomprehension.

"Mrs. Harper, you said you had heard Mr. Berger's truck that morning—the morning the apartment was vandalized—and you thought he was delivering the linens."

"Yes, but obviously he must have been collecting them," Mrs. Harper said.

Pauline shook her head. "He couldn't have been, because he collected them two days earlier. I remember, because he and I had a little chat about the German language for some, er, research I was doing." Research for her current novel, since Emma Daring's adversary in this one was a former German soldier made bitter by his country's loss in the war, and Pauline had wanted to make sure she got the bits of German interspersed with his English correct.

Mrs. Harper's brow wrinkled as she tried to figure this out. "But if he'd already collected the linens, and he wasn't delivering them, what was he doing here that day?"

That was the question indeed.

A letter from Miss Lewis to the Bergers, one so important the former schoolteacher wanted it delivered by hand. The laundry truck heard both at the murder scene and Pauline's apartment.

Things were not looking good for Heinrich Berger. Yet Pauline still could not believe that kindly man could harm anyone, much less commit murder.

"Thank you, Mrs. Harper, Mr. Denney," she said, hardly knowing what she was saying. "Good day."

The gloves and stockings would have to wait. She needed to know what Mr. Berger had said to James.

Pauline walked the rest of the way to the police station without seeing any of the scenery or even the people she passed. Her mind worked furiously. There had to be a mistake somewhere. The pieces seemed to all fit together... but the picture wasn't right. She simply couldn't put her finger on why it was wrong.

That bothered her almost as much as the thought of Heinrich Berger being a murderer. Pauline solved her puzzles through logic and deduction, not instinct and hunches. So why did she feel so certain things didn't add up here? There had to be a reason, if only she could work her way toward it.

James was in the police station, located in the lower levels of the Opera House, when Pauline arrived. His face was set in lines of weariness and frustration, echoing her own feelings.

"Heinrich Berger says his truck was 'not available for his use' that morning, but he won't say why or in what way," he greeted her abruptly. "His wife says the same, and she also won't give a clear answer. The darn thing about it is I'm tempted to believe them. They seem to be protecting somebody, but who? Mrs. Berger's sister? I can't see them being willing to risk Berger going to jail for anyone less than family, but neither can I see Miss Hertz committing murder."

Pauline's own face felt dragged down by her worry. "It gets worse." She told him her own news from Mrs. Harper and Mr. Denney.

James rubbed his forehead. "So the murderer—whoever it was—drove to Miss Lewis's house in the truck, killed her, ransacked the house for whatever-it-was he was looking for, and when he didn't find it drove over to your house to search there for it, and then calmly drove back to the Bergers' place and... did what? If it was Berger or one of the womenfolk, did they just go back to their normal routine? If it was someone else that they are protecting, where is that person now, and why in tarnation would the Bergers be protecting them?"

"Have you searched the truck?"

James nodded. "We confiscated it. Wallace is going over it with a fine tooth comb now. The chief thinks we ought to arrest Berger now, that there's enough evidence pointing to him as our culprit that motive doesn't matter."

Pauline shook her head mutely, but couldn't think up an argument against it.

"Of course, if what Denney said is true—and it likely is, knowing him—that could give us our motive. Pity we couldn't find that letter, but no doubt the killer destroyed it. Still, I'll have the chief contact the Saratoga Springs police and we'll find that Janet Arden, and she ought to be able to tell us herself what was in the letter. It's only a matter of time now before the motive comes to light." James rose from his chair, stretched, and reached for his jacket. "For now, let's go home. There's not much more I can do here now."

The trip back to the house was silent. Pauline was still trying to think of a way to explain away everything pointing to Mr. Berger as the killer, and James didn't seem inclined toward conversation, either. As they entered the farmhouse, he at last cleared his throat and spoke again.

"I know you don't like to think of Berger as a murderer, Pauline, but at this point I don't see how we can justify looking for anyone else. The chief wants this settled, and everything points to Berger." He shifted his eyes to avoid Pauline's gaze. "Enough people here remember the war that it won't go overly well with him if it goes to trial. Most folk like the Bergers, but it would be easier to blame a German than to admit one of us could have committed such a violent and senseless murder."

Pauline's lips pressed into a thin line. "And here I thought this was one place that rose above that sort of narrow-minded prejudice. I suppose that means I'm not really 'one of you' either? Not unless our parents and grandparents were born here, is that it?"

"That's not what I meant!" James protested, but he still wouldn't meet Pauline's eyes.

Ruby had entered the foyer by this point, wanting to see what was keeping her husband and their guest. She shook her head and rested a hand on Pauline's sleeve. "That isn't entirely fair, my friend. Yes, we have our share of prejudices here, who doesn't?" She smiled ruefully. "My grandmother had a few stories to tell about the difficulties of being an Iroquois woman married to a white man. My mother had to put up with her share of whispers and snubbing. But I barely ever hear a whisper about my ancestry. Sometimes things do improve." She sighed. "Sometimes they don't. I don't think there's any place or person that lives up to its own ideals. But isn't the important thing that we keep trying?"

Pauline released a breath and her anger at the same time. Ruby was right, of course. She wished she weren't, but there was no place on earth that was perfect. Overall, the good still outweighed the bad here.

"Thank you," she said.

Then she frowned. Something Ruby had said has sparked a vague notion in her brain. What was it?

Unreasonable prejudice... whispers and snubs... the way things used to be...

Nothing hung together yet, but she thought that perhaps somewhere in the murky dimness they had been stumbling through so far a little light was starting to glimmer.

"James, I don't know who it is Mr. Berger is protecting, or why, but I am convinced that he is innocent, as are Mrs. Berger and Miss Hertz."

Before he could answer, yet another new figure appeared at the open door, and a new voice joined the conversation.

"I am pleased to hear you say that, Miss Gray. I believe I can give some explanation of my brother-in-law's silence."

106

CHAPTER 11
New Information

Miss Klara Hertz stood before them, dressed in her Sunday best of a navy suit with a crisp white blouse beneath and a Panama hat covering her hair. She turned her attention to Ruby before anyone could react.

"I apologize for coming in unannounced, Mrs. Richardson, but I am in great distress for my brother-in-law."

Ruby recovered her aplomb. "Of course, Miss Hertz. You have no need to apologize. Please, come in."

She ushered the three of them into the little-used parlor and vanished back into the kitchen, likely to see if her supper could be saved and stretched for an extra guest. Miss Hertz sat on the extreme edge of the horsehair sofa, her back ramrod straight. She didn't do anything so gauche as twist a handkerchief in her hands, but by their very stillness as they lay folded in her lap she gave evidence of her distress. Pauline didn't think she'd ever seen Miss Hertz when her hands were still—she was always busy at some task or another, mending or knitting or chopping vegetables or weeding the garden. It seemed wrong for her hands to be so idle.

"My sister and brother believe his truck was borrowed by the Addison and Ingersoll children that morning, and they do not wish to get them in trouble for a harmless prank," she began abruptly.

James whipped out his notepad and pencil and began furiously scribbling. "Hold on a minute there, Miss Hertz. Start at the beginning."

Miss Hertz drew in a deep breath and obliged. "That morning, when Heinrich went to do his usual round, the truck was gone. You know we are neighbors to both the Addisons and the Ingersolls, yes?"

"I do," Pauline put in. "I saw your sister at the Ingersolls this morning when I was out there. And—yes, she *did* say the children had played a nasty trick on her husband the morning of the murder."

James turned his head to look at her. "That would have been helpful for you to remember before," he commented mildly.

"But I didn't know it was in relation to the truck," she protested. "Not until just now. One doesn't tend to associate childish pranks with a stolen truck, murder, and attempted theft."

He acknowledged this with a nod and they both turned their attention back to Miss Hertz.

"Mrs. Addison and Mrs. Ingersoll take it in turns to watch each other's children once a week so the other lady can do her grocery shopping and other such things in peace. The youngsters are always in some sort of mischief when they get together. You know how children are."

James had to smooth away a reminiscent smile as he nodded in agreement, likely recalling some of his own childhood pranks.

"The eldest Ingersoll boy has been driving a tractor since before he was old enough to reach the pedals and see out the front at the same time. He considers himself an expert driver by this point. He 'borrowed' Heinrich's truck once before. His father punished him severely for it, and he said he would never do it again, but when Heinrich went out and saw that the truck was gone, and recalled that it was the day for Mrs. Addison to watch all the children, he believed they must have taken it again. As it was returned later in the day with no scratches or damage, he decided not to say anything. Now he does not wish to put the children under suspicion, so he continues to say nothing."

"But you don't agree," James said.

Miss Hertz's eyes were a very deep, very calm blue. She turned them on James as she answered, "I do not wish to protect anyone at the expense of my brother-in-law's life. He is a good man. But also I do not agree that the children were the ones to take the truck, and so I do not consider that I am endangering them by speaking."

"Who do you think took it, then?" James asked, pencil poised eagerly.

"I do not know. But I did not think it was the children even at the time."

"Why not?" Pauline spoke up, genuinely curious. She didn't either, mostly because the boys had told her they hadn't played any trick on Mr. Berger that day, but she wondered what Miss Hertz's reasoning was. Perhaps it wasn't strictly relevant to the matter at hand, but she wanted to know.

Miss Hertz turned to her. "Because they did it once. They do not like to repeat themselves, those young ones. A trick played once and paid for in full is a trick that is no longer amusing."

Pauline didn't know much about children, but that seemed like sound logic, and it fit with what the lads had told her. From the way James was nodding it appeared he agreed as well.

"Can you tell me anything about when and how the truck was returned?" he asked now.

Miss Hertz shook her head. "It must have been in the middle of luncheon. When we sat down to eat, the truck was not there, and when we left the table, it was. The kitchen is at the back of the house, so we would not have seen or heard anyone bringing it back."

"A pity," James said. "Perhaps the Addisons or Ingersolls might know more—or no, not Mrs. Ingersoll. She would have been out running errands, correct? Mrs. Addison, then."

He stopped speaking abruptly, and his eyes met Pauline's over Miss Hertz's head. She guessed that the same notion that had struck her had also struck him.

Mrs. Ingersoll...?

Pauline's brain shifted into sensational novelist mode. What if the farm didn't properly belong to the Ingersolls? What if Tom Martens had left it to Anita Lewis in his will, and they had obtained it through underhanded means? What if the letter from Janet Arden contained proof of that? Would they kill in order to keep their home?

Farmers all over the country were losing their livelihoods, more and more every day. So far most folk in this region had managed to hang on, but it was getting harder and harder. A person absolutely might kill in order to protect their family's heritage, especially if the victim were an old woman and they could justify it to themselves by saying she was going to die soon anyway.

They might have thought themselves safe for years, until Pauline spoke at the sewing bee about the memoirs. Then Mrs. Ingersoll might have panicked, thinking the truth might be coming out after all these years, and that they had to stop the memoirs from going forward at all costs.

If Mr. Ingersoll was at the farm all day, then Mrs. Ingersoll would have been the one to do it. Deliver the children to her neighbor, steal the truck, drive to Miss Lewis's, hit her over the head, hurriedly search for the letter, leave due to the milkman coming, head to Pauline's on the chance that the letter might have ended up with her, and then back to drop the truck at the Bergers and collect her children in time for lunch.

Could a woman truly do that?

It seemed unfathomable, but Pauline knew that mothers could do almost anything when it came to protecting their children.

But then how could she have been so calm and collected when Pauline was there earlier? She certainly didn't act like a woman with a guilty conscience. Was she really that talented at dissembling? She had seemed so pleased at the idea of Pauline continuing with Miss Lewis's memoirs. If she was guilty, how could she be so composed?

And good heavens, if she were the murderer, how could they ever prove it?

"Miss Hertz," Pauline said, "did Mr. Denney deliver a note to anyone in your family from Miss Lewis the day before she was killed?"

Miss Hertz shook her head. "No. Had she written to us? Perhaps the letter was lost. The mail had been disrupted and was covered in mud when Mr. Denney did bring it to us."

"What are you thinking, Pauline?" James asked.

"You need to talk to Mr. Denney again," Pauline said. "Our conversation was interrupted by Mrs. Harper. He didn't actually say the note was to the Bergers, only that he had it in his hand when he was knocked into at their house." The garrulous old man enjoyed telling his stories, and could quite easily have been leading up to saying that the note was for Mrs. Ingersoll and he had only gotten ready to hand-deliver it to her at the Bergers.

"And what will you be doing?"

"I need to visit Mr. Crane once more." If the letter was the proof, then Pauline's notes had nothing to do with why her apartment was searched. And if *that* was the case that meant that the killer hadn't found the letter and destroyed it after all. Which meant that either Miss Lewis herself had destroyed it, or else it was still hidden somewhere in her house.

Saratoga Springs was a large city. It could take a long time for the police there to track down Janet Arden, and even then there was no guarantee she would be willing to tell them what was in her letter. Besides, what if she was a visitor to the area, not a resident? If there was any way to get the letter itself, they needed to take it.

James frowned. "You shouldn't be visiting him on your own, even if we are mostly certain he isn't the murderer. You aren't even supposed to be involved in this investigation!"

"I will accompany Miss Gray," announced Miss Hertz, rising to her feet. "If you say your chief wants to wrap this case up quickly even if it means blaming an innocent man, then it will take those of us who are not under his authority to discover the truth."

Pauline couldn't have stated it any better.

"How do I get myself into these sorts of messes?" James muttered with a sigh. "Very well. Just... please, be safe, ladies."

Pauline had cause to be thankful for the long June days as she and Miss Hertz left on their bicycles. She had a headlamp, but she was still nervous about cycling after dark.

Miss Hertz took the lead, and Pauline realized she was an expert on a bicycle. Her legs pumped smoothly and strongly, and she pulled well ahead of Pauline without the slightest appearance of strain. Proof, if any was needed, that she wouldn't have had to use her brother's truck if she'd wanted to get to Miss Lewis's house. She could have managed the bicycle ride with ease.

As she followed the older woman, Pauline's mind was free to range over the case again. The pieces seemed to be fitting together, but something was still not quite right. That idea that had started to emerge earlier, about prejudice and propriety and shunning... what had it been? It had been interrupted by Miss Hertz's arrival and everything seeming to point to Mrs. Ingersoll and the farm, but where had it been leading? Pauline couldn't help but feel somehow they had gotten off track.

There was something else, something about a girl, a girl who had stayed with Miss Lewis after bring thrown out of her family's house. Yes, that was right! Mrs. Addison had spoken about it, as had the vicar's wife. An unwed mother, so Pauline had gathered from what wasn't said. Shocking and shameful, but Miss Lewis had taken her in out of kindness.

Now, why had she remembered that? What was it about that story that struck her as important? Surely that girl couldn't be connected to this death. So why had it come to mind when Pauline was thinking about secrets and shame? There had been no secret about that girl's child, clearly.

Pauline's thoughts scattered again as Miss Hertz expertly swooped to a stop in front of Miss Lewis's house. Pauline glanced at the big brick MacNeill house as she stopped behind Miss Hertz. Mrs. MacNeill was in her front garden, puttering about. She gave a little wave to Pauline, and didn't even pretend to not be watching them with avid curiosity.

Pauline returned the wave and looked in the other direction, toward the County Home and the few cows grazing on the field between that and Miss Lewis's house. They couldn't be making a mistake, could they? What if everything really was as simple as a man looking to escape the shame of the poorhouse, and willing to commit violence to do so?

There was that word again. *Shame.* Why did it keep sticking in her mind?

No time to dwell on it now—Mr. Crane had come out the front door to greet them.

"Welcome, ladies!" he said, his head tilted to one side a little quizzically. "It seems all of Canton wishes to pay its condolences on behalf of my aunt today. Mrs. Ingersoll and Mrs. Addison are already inside. Won't you join us?"

Mrs. Ingersoll! Pauline's heart jumped. Then the letter *must* be the key. It couldn't be a coincidence that she was here now. She must be attempting to find it before Mr. Crane could.

"Splendid," Miss Hertz said calmly. "Come, Miss Gray."

Pauline never would have imagined herself obeying someone else's command, but to her own astonishment she found herself trailing meekly after Miss Hertz even while her mind raced feverishly to try to concoct a plan for getting that letter before Mrs. Ingersoll could.

She only hoped it wasn't too late already.

CHAPTER TWELVE
Questions Answered

It was with mixed feelings that Pauline found herself walking through the front door of Miss Lewis's house. She had never come in this way before—always through the back, into the kitchen. As Mr. Crane ushered them into the living room, Pauline thought of how pleased Miss Lewis had been to show her this room, and even more so the library beyond it. No doubt Mr. Crane, who had so little time for reading, would dispose of all the books his aunt had collected so painstakingly over the years before he sold the house. What a loss!

To her surprise, Pauline did not feel haunted or squeamish as she walked into the very room where Miss Lewis had met her end. Indeed, the house felt very much as it always had: warm and welcoming, as though its owner was still hovering in it to make her guests comfortable, somewhere just out of sight. Insensibly, Pauline felt her mind calm and her nerves steady even as her eyes fell on Mrs. Ingersoll in one of the wing-backed chairs, with Mrs. Addison tucked into the other. She almost felt Miss Lewis pat her on the shoulder, encouraging her for the task to come.

"It was lucky for all you ladies that you came today," Mr. Crane said, showing Miss Hertz and Pauline to the small sofa. He left the room briefly and returned with a wooden chair from the dining room, sitting on that so as to leave the more comfortable seats for his guests. "I finished my inventory of the house just this morning, and I'll be putting everything up for auction as soon as the police say I may."

An auction! Pauline's heart sank. All of Miss Lewis's precious memories, scattered across the county to people who cared only for their monetary value. She sternly returned her thoughts to the matter at hand.

"You must have found a great many interesting items in your aunt's possessions," Miss Hertz said. "She led such a full life."

"A simple and quiet one, if you ask me," Mr. Crane corrected her. "A few trinkets saved from her parents and grandparents, or given to her by her students, and more books than anyone could ever read in a lifetime. No, I doubt it will bring much at auction, but every little bit helps." He sighed heavily, though none of the women present seemed inclined to share in his self-pity.

How could Pauline bring the conversation around to Miss Lewis's papers without alerting Mrs. Ingersoll? Where would Miss Lewis have been most likely to store the letter?

"I should dearly like to see her books," Miss Hertz continued. "I do not read much, myself—there is always so much work to do!—but sometimes, I do enjoy a good book. In winter, *ja*, when the time has slowed? One cannot knit all the time, after all."

The other women laughed, and Pauline marveled at how well her companion was doing.

"Of course!" said Mr. Crane, springing up and crossing to the library door. "All of you, come in and look, if you like."

"Actually, Mr. Crane, what I would most like to see would be some of Miss Lewis's old photos," said Mrs. Ingersoll. Pauline, about to enter the library, halted abruptly. Old photos...?

Mrs. Ingersoll continued. "Cathy and I were just talking about it on our way here—how Miss Lewis kept so many photographs of all her students, and how we'd like to remember our time with her as our teacher."

Now why would Mrs. Ingersoll want old photographs? Unless that was an excuse, just as the books were for Miss Hertz, and she wanted a chance to rummage around looking for the letter. Or was there another reason?

"Naturally," said Mr. Crane. "Of course you would! Aunt Anita kept most of her photographs in the library as well."

Most of them... but not all. Pauline distinctly remembered Miss Lewis showing her a photo of her former students that she kept in the dining room. She opened her mouth to say so—and then closed it again. What if there really was another reason for wanting an old photograph?

Pauline hung back as the others went into the library, with Mr. Crane leading the way. Mrs. Addison stopped before entering, waving to Pauline to go on ahead of her.

"No, no," Pauline murmured, inclining her head and hoping it would be taken for politeness—the younger woman allowing her elders to go first. "After you, Mrs. Addison."

"No, please," said Mrs. Addison. "You must be terribly fond of books, after all. I'm such a dunce, there's little there to interest me."

The battle of courtesies was broken by Mrs. Ingersoll.

"Oh Cathy, come and look! Here's one from when we were just starting at the high school. Goodness, how scrawny you were! Why do I always remember you as plump?"

Slowly, reluctantly, Mrs. Addison walked into the library to obey Mrs. Ingersoll's imperative summons. Pauline waited only a heartbeat or two more, just long enough to ensure no one was watching her through the open doorway, and then darted into the dining room to look at the whatnot.

Yes, there it was, just as she remembered, a silver-framed photograph of one of Miss Lewis's final classes. Only it wasn't exactly as she remembered—it was crooked in the frame, as though it had been removed and replaced clumsily. Pauline recalled Miss Lewis's comments on her arthritic fingers. What if she had placed something behind the photo in the frame, and had not been able to put the photograph back as neatly as she would have wished?

Moving quickly now, no dithering or doubt hindering her actions, Pauline turned the frame over to remove the back. A thrill zipped through her body as the back came away to reveal a neatly folded piece of stationery. Pauline carefully set the frame down on the whatnot and unfolded the paper. She glanced first at the signature: *Janet Arden.*

She had found the letter.

It had been Pauline's intention to slip the letter into her handbag and turn it over to James without reading it—she recoiled from the idea of reading someone else's private correspondence, and it was the police's business, not hers—but now that it came down to it, she couldn't help herself.

Dear Miss Lewis,

Please forgive a stranger for writing to you like this, but I do not know where else to turn. My mother passed away last month, and left me a letter informing me that I was adopted as a baby, and that you were the woman who arranged the adoption. I would like to find the woman who gave me birth—

Before Pauline had a chance to read any further, a sharp voice interrupted her.

"What are you doing with that? Is that a letter? Where did you get that? Give it to me!"

Pauline looked up to see—not Mrs. Ingersoll, but Mrs. Addison, advancing on her with an outstretched hand and a pinched look on her face as she glanced from the stationery in Pauline right hand to the photograph frame in her left.

"Give me that letter!" she repeated. Pauline clutched the letter close to her chest and backed away, mind spinning.

Mrs. Addison...?

Scraps of conversation and memories began falling into place in her mind. Mrs. Ingersoll commenting on how skinny Cathy Addison was at the start of their high school years, yet her memories of her were always of her being plump... hearing after the sewing bee how strict Mrs. Addison's parents had been... Mrs. Addison blindly defending her son to Officer Wallace... Miss Lewis taking in a young unwed mother despite the scandal of it all... the Ingersoll boys eagerly telling how they and the Addison boys had been allowed to play unsupervised the morning of the murder...

Not Mrs. Ingersoll trying to protect her family's farm. Not any of the Bergers for reasons unknown. Not Mrs. MacNeill or her son, not Samuel Crane.

No, the heart of this crime was Mrs. Addison, protecting a deep and scandalous secret that she could never let out for fear of the damage it would do to her reputation, the fear of losing her husband's respect and her sons' love. Even if, as their friends and neighbors claimed, they all loved her blindly and devotedly, her upbringing meant that she could never quite trust that love. So she would do anything, even kill, to keep it, and to keep her upright reputation in town.

While all this was whirling through Pauline's mind, Mrs. Addison had snatched up the poker from the fireplace and was brandishing it at Pauline.

"*Give me the letter,*" she repeated again, her voice low and hard.

For one horrible moment, Pauline almost complied, so urgent was the demand, but her body was moving away before her mind caught up. If this was Miss Lewis's murderer, no matter what her motivation—no, Pauline could not let her escape justice, no matter what the cost to herself!

Pauline thought she knew now what the rest of the letter said, but she couldn't give it up—it was the only scrap of evidence that existed against Cathy Addison for Miss Lewis's murder. Though the fact that Mrs. Addison was willing to attack her with a poker in front of witnesses might stand as evidence enough, she supposed.

Those witnesses now spilled out of the library to stare at the scene playing out before their eyes: Pauline, breath coming quickly and a mist rising up before her eyes, stumbling over her own feet as she moved backward from the relentlessly advancing Mrs. Addison.

"My dear madam!" blustered Mr. Crane. "What on earth is the matter?"

"Cathy, for heaven's sake!" Mrs. Ingersoll chimed in.

Mrs. Addison paid no attention to either of them. She continued menacing Pauline, who was now backed right up against the wall, letter clutched to her chest, with nowhere else to go.

Miss Hertz wasted neither time nor breath in remonstrating. She took two long strides to reach Mrs. Addison's side, and with her strong hands wrenched the poker away from the other woman. Mrs. Addison whirled on her.

"No!" she shrieked. "I have to have it! No one must read it! No one must know!" She turned back to Pauline, eyes glittering and cheeks bright red, and attacked with only her bare hands, striking indiscriminately as she tried to wrench the paper from Pauline's grasp. "Give it to me, you interfering busybody! Why did you have to come poking your nose into everything?"

Under normal circumstances, Pauline could have fended off the wild attack, but she was hampered by her need to protect the letter from being torn. She hunched in on herself, curling her entire body around the letter she still clutched in her hand, head ducked down in an attempt to escape the worst of the blows. In her dizzied mind was only one thought: justice for Miss Lewis.

"Call the police," she heard Miss Hertz command, and then she was freed from the attack, uncurling to see Miss Hertz holding Mrs. Addison with her arms pinioned at her sides. Even now, Mrs. Addison struggled to free herself, kicking Miss Hertz's shins and attempting to wrench loose. Mr. Crane was nowhere in sight—presumably he had obeyed Miss Hertz's order to telephone the police—and Mrs. Ingersoll stood frozen, hands pressed to her mouth in horror.

"Mrs. Addison," Pauline began, and stopped, helplessly. What could she say?

"I have nothing to say to you," Mrs. Addison snarled. "You have no right to go snooping about in other people's affairs!"

Pauline swallowed and began again. "We all have things we're ashamed of." She was thinking not only of Mrs. Addison's secret then, but her own, but Mrs. Addison reacted before she could say anything more.

"You don't know what you're talking about! How dare you? Be quiet!"

Pauline would have liked to be quiet, but she couldn't. However ugly this was, the truth had to be told. "Miss Anita Lewis knew the secret you were keeping, didn't she? In fact, she was the one who enabled you to keep it a secret. But you couldn't let it rest. The knowledge ate away at you, and it started twisting you up inside. Instead of trusting that your secret was safe with Miss Lewis, you started believing that knowing that secret gave her power over you. You were afraid, afraid that someday she might tell the truth. Perhaps she would even tell it to the journalist who was helping her write her memoirs. Perhaps those memoirs would be published, and then everyone would know the truth. The secret would no longer be safe."

Pauline held up the letter. Mrs. Addison lunged forward again, only to come up short against Miss Hertz's unyielding grip. "That might not have been enough on its own for you to kill her. But then this letter arrived. A letter, I believe, from a daughter looking for the mother who had given her up many years ago. The daughter didn't know who that mother was, but she did know the name of the woman who helped her mother—Miss Lewis. And so she wrote, asking Miss Lewis for her mother's identity. Miss Lewis in turn sent you a note, telling you of the letter and asking to speak with you about it." This last bit was guesswork, but it made sense, and Pauline didn't want to show Mrs. Addison just how shaky the foundation of this reconstruction was. She believed this was how it had to have played out, but if she started asking questions to confirm her belief rather than stating facts, Mrs. Addison still might try to twist out of the truth.

"And so you came, early in the morning, sending your boys out to play with the Ingersoll lads, using Heinrich Berger's truck so no one would know it was you, and you killed Miss Lewis in order to prevent her from ever revealing the truth to your daughter, or anyone else."

"No!" Mrs. Addison said.

"You left our boys unsupervised?" Mrs. Ingersoll demanded, latching onto the least important revelation. "How could you?"

"No," Mrs. Addison repeated. "I was home all morning. I wasn't here!"

"You were not home," Miss Hertz contradicted. "I walked across the road after Heinrich's truck went missing and knocked on your door to ask if you saw who took it, and you were not there."

Mrs. Ingersoll blinked.

"*You?*" Mrs. Ingersoll whispered. "You let our children play together in the woods while you went and–*killed* her? You killed Miss Lewis? Why? For heaven's sake, why?"

Speech poured out of Mrs. Addison all at once like water from a fountain, and she jabbed her chin in Pauline's direction. "It was her fault, not mine! That Miss Gray, always poking her nose in other people's business. All these years, Miss Lewis kept my secret, but she was getting old, her memory was getting shaky, how could I trust that she wouldn't forget how important it was? What if she slipped? Then she sent me that note, telling me about the letter. I couldn't risk it. What if she decided it was her duty to tell? I would have lost everything! I had to do it. I had to. She was old, she would have died soon enough anyway. It's not my fault. None of it has been my fault. I didn't want the baby in the first place. I was just a girl! I didn't understand. I trusted Miss Lewis to make it go away. She helped me hide it from my family and everyone else, had me go stay with a friend of hers downstate for the last few months and the birth. She even found a home for the baby after it was born. I thought I could trust her, I thought it was safe. But I couldn't risk it. I couldn't risk her telling about it. What would everyone think? What would my husband say? What about my boys? I would be shamed forever. I had to do it. I didn't have a choice. It was all her fault." She sneered at Pauline. "Why couldn't you have stayed in Albany where you belong?"

With one brutal twist, she wrenched herself from Miss Hertz's grasp. But this time she didn't come for Pauline—instead she lunged for the front door, pulling it open and racing outside. The other three women tripped over each other in their dash to follow, with Mr. Crane on their heels. They heard a wild wail and the screech of a braking automobile, but only Miss Hertz was close enough to the open door to see what happened.

"Ach, it is the police! They have nearly run her over... no, she escaped, and she is running across the field toward the river. Lieutenant Richardson is chasing her, as is the younger one."

Pauline abruptly turned away. She didn't want to see what she was afraid was about to happen.

"The river?" Mrs. Ingersoll whispered. "But Cathy can't swim..."

Was it Pauline's imagination, or did she hear a splash, as of someone jumping into the water?

"Lieutenant Richardson has jumped in after her," Miss Hertz confirmed. She turned aside and closed the door. "But I do not think he will be able to save her."

Mr. Crane mopped his forehead with his handkerchief. "Bless my soul," he said in a shaking voice. "Bless my soul."

James and Wallace returned to the house a short time later, dripping wet and somber with the news that they could not save Mrs. Addison, and there was no more time for reflection as the story had to be told once more, and the letter, at last, handed over for safekeeping to the police.

"I remember now," Mrs. Ingersoll said in a quiet voice. "I remember that summer. We all thought Cathy had gotten fat as the school year ended, but none of us knew why. Nor did we ever question it when she had slimmed down by the time fall came. She did change after that, though. She'd been full of fun before then, but after that she was quieter, more withdrawn. Why did we never put it all together? And this poor soul—her daughter, you say, Miss Gray?—she only wanted to find her mother, and instead drove her to murder. Oh dear, oh dear."

"If murder was what she was willing to do to protect herself from shame, it would have happened regardless," Miss Hertz said in a hard voice. "No one else is responsible for Mrs. Addison's actions, save she alone."

Pauline couldn't quite agree with that sentiment. Yes, ultimately responsibility rested on Mrs. Addison's shoulders. But the way she was raised must have played a role in her actions, as well as the sure knowledge that she would have been shunned by the community should her deed ever come to light. What was that John Donne quote? 'No man is an island entire of itself.'

In a way, they all had a hand in shaping each other. Miss Lewis's kindness had rippled out and brought peace and comfort to an entire community... and darker deeds brought loss and sorrow to the community as well. Deeds that sprouted and spread in the hotbed of secrecy and untruth.

Before she could think better of it, Pauline opened her mouth and spoke. "I know something of having a secret you wish to protect."

She had thought she would never reveal this to anyone, but Mrs. Hansen had been right when she spoke about secrets at the sewing bee. Secrets were poisonous. It was time to clear away the poison from Pauline's own life, and help all of them recover from the shock and horror of Mrs. Addison's desperate deeds.

"Shortly after my graduation from college, I found myself in a dilemma," she continued. "I had very few job prospects, and my choices seemed to be either find a husband or move back home to be with my parents. I did not want to do either—I loved this town and wanted to stay here, and I was not prepared to take on the responsibilities of being a housewife, even if someone had asked me to marry him, which in any case did not happen."

Mrs. Ingersoll leaned forward and patted her knee. "Give it time, dearie. With a pretty face like yours, you won't have to worry for long about being an old maid!"

Pauline drew in a deep breath and continued, ignoring this mistaken attempt at sympathy. She knew well enough that very few people believed she genuinely did not want a husband. That was not the point of this story. "I applied for a position at the *Watertown Daily Times*, but even if they accepted me, I knew my salary there would not be enough to live on. What I wanted to do more than anything was serious writing, academic writing. I loved to research different topics and then write about them; it was by far my favorite part of college. But it is not so easy to make a living from that, especially not if one is a woman. I was visiting a friend one day and happened to glance at the adventure novel her thirteen-year-old son was reading. 'I could do better than that,' I thought, and the next moment, I decided I would try, at least until something better came along."

Pauline could not believe she was about to do this. The only other person in the world who knew her secret was Sarah, who did not entirely understand why Pauline was so ashamed of her novels but respected her desire to keep them private. She pressed on.

"I dashed off a story in a few weeks and sent it to an editor, never thinking anything might come of it. To my shock, the editor wrote back and said he not only wanted to publish it, he would like to turn it into a series. At first I refused to consider it. I didn't think it was the kind of writing I ought to be doing. Not that there was any harm in it—I wouldn't write anything like that—but that it wasn't academic enough. But it paid enough that I could pay rent and buy groceries, and so I signed the contract, but refused to affix my real name to the books. Aside from my roommate, no one else has ever known that I am the author of the Emma Daring books."

James slapped his knee. "Ha! I knew you were hiding something all these years. I'll admit, I never guessed that, though. Well done, Pauline."

Mrs. Ingersoll gasped, but she didn't seem shocked or horrified. "Why, my Charlie loves your books!" she blurted out. "Why wouldn't you tell people?"

"I kept it a secret all this time because I was ashamed," Pauline explained. "I didn't want my former professors and fellow students to know I was writing what all of us would have considered 'tripe.' And the longer I kept it a secret, the more important it became to continue to keep it a secret. That's what secrets do. They take over your life and take on a monumental importance, and eventually you will be willing to do almost anything to keep them buried. Just like Mrs. Addison."

That sobered her listeners, reminding them of the real reason they were all here.

"Willing to murder," James said. "And not only that, but to cast blame on others. Miss Hertz, I believe we owe your brother an apology."

"It was a logical assumption, given everything," the German woman said graciously. "I am not entirely certain of one thing, though—did she burglarize Miss Gray's home to find her memoir notes or look for the letter?"

"Both, I would think," James said. "Since she couldn't find the letter here, she thought she'd check there and make sure there was nothing in the notes that could give away her secret. Well, well, it's a sad story all the way around. Mr. Crane, we'll leave you to your home now."

"Er—yes," Mr. Crane said, still shaken by it all. "Thank you. Goodness me, how will I ever find a buyer now?" he exclaimed, as though struck by the sudden thought. "First Aunt Anita, and then her murderer? It will have a terrible reputation! No one will want to live here!"

In the midst of her weariness and sorrow, it seemed Pauline still had room for grief over that thought. Despite the ugliness that had happened here, she still loved this home—the peace that Miss Lewis had spread from here far outweighed the violence that had happened. Even if Pauline had believed in ghosts, she would have known instinctively that there could be no unhappy ghosts haunting this home.

A thought brushed across her mind. At first she dismissed it as not appropriate for the moment, but it returned, and at last she promised herself she would consider it more carefully once everything was settled. Perhaps this home did not need to be abandoned to decay and loneliness after all.

Outside, James turned to Pauline. "You were both right and wrong about Al Denney. Right in that the note wasn't for the Bergers, but it wasn't for Mrs. Ingersoll, either. It was for Mrs. Addison. I was just about ready to come out here anyway to see if you'd found the letter when Crane telephoned the station. Wallace and I got out here as quick as we could. Not quick enough, as it turned out." He sighed. "Still, I suppose Mrs. Addison preferred it this way. She spared her family the shame of seeing her on trial. And from what you say, I don't think she could have lived with the knowledge that her secret was revealed to the world."

"No," Pauline said softly. "I don't think she could."

"Speaking of secrets..." James said, making a visible effort to shake off his grim mood. "I can't believe you never told any of us that you are a famous author! I did wonder about seeing those papers on your floor, but you were so gol-darned insistent on your privacy I didn't allow myself to speculate. Say, Jeremy is going to be thrilled. He loves those Emma Daring stories. For that matter, I've been known to enjoy one on a Sunday afternoon myself."

"I think they're swell!" blurted Officer Wallace. "In fact, uh..."

"Spit it out, Wallace," James said good-naturedly.

Wallace reached into the backseat of the police car and pulled out a paperback novel, the cover of which featured a young woman in trousers and a motoring coat crossing a deep chasm on a rickety rope bridge while a villain fired at her from behind some boulders on the far side. He held it out to Pauline and blurted,

"Would you mind signing this for me? It's my favorite."

Pauline wasn't sure whether she should laugh or cry. In the end, she did neither. Instead, she pulled her ever-present pen from the bottom of her handbag, and for the first time in her life, gravely signed her name across the front page of an Emma Daring novel.

CHAPTER THIRTEEN
A New Beginning

Three months passed before Pauline stood in front of Miss Lewis's house again. This time she wasn't alone. Sarah, long since returned from her visit to her family in Philadelphia, stood beside her, and Klara Hertz was on her other side. Behind them was Heinrich Berger's old truck filled with boxes of their possessions and a few small pieces of furniture. Though the roses were long since past, the asters shone like purple stars in the mellow golden light of late summer, and the apples on the tree in the backyard were starting to blush rosily as they moved toward ripeness.

A great deal had happened in the preceding weeks. After long arguments with herself, and even longer discussions with Sarah, Pauline had finally approached the bank about a loan to purchase a house. The revelation of her identity as the author of the Emma Daring novels had, surprisingly, helped her here. With the assurance of the books bringing her in a steady income, even more than her newspaper column, the bank had been happy to loan her the necessary money.

The next step was approaching Samuel Crane. He had been so relieved at the thought of a buyer who wasn't frightened away by the violent death that had happened in the house that he had let it go for a relative song. It seemed his irritation the day Pauline had spoken to him about his aunt's death had been at the prospect of being saddled with a house he couldn't sell because no one would feel comfortable in it.

Next Pauline had contracted a builder to add a small addition to one side of the house, just enough for one more bedroom, this one on the ground floor.

When the builders finally finished, Miss Hertz, Mrs. Berger, and Mrs. MacNeill came in with such an array of buckets, rags, mops, and cleaning solutions that it made Pauline's head spin. Those good women refused to take any payment for their work, saying it was the least they could do to thank Pauline for searching past the obvious and discovering the truth of the murder.

And now, at last, it was ready.

Her very own home.

At first, Pauline had wanted Sarah to co-own the house, but her friend had refused.

"Someday I might want to get married, and then we'd have the bother of having to settle which one of us got the house, and that one buying it from the other," she pointed out. "And frankly, I'm not sure I like the idea of the responsibility of being a homeowner. I'd much rather leave it to my landlord—or landlady—to take care of house repairs and the hundred and one little things that always need taking care of in a house." She grinned at her friend.

Then Pauline had offered to simply let Sarah live there and share in daily expenses, but Sarah would have none of that, either.

"If I stay, I pay my own way, same as I have done here," she said firmly.

Pauline was stubborn, but Sarah was more stubborn yet, and so in the end, Pauline yielded. Sarah had the second upstairs bedroom and paid Pauline for room and board. In truth, the money was welcome, as Pauline was indeed finding that being a homeowner was already putting more strain on her purse than she had anticipated.

The third member of their new trio was the reason for the builders. Pauline was determined to keep this house as lovely as Miss Lewis had made it, and she knew she was not capable of doing so on her own, nor even with Sarah, as both were working women and neither was inclined to give up her leisure hours to housework. Pauline recalled Mrs. Berger speaking of her sister's restlessness in living with them as well as Miss Hertz's own admission that she did not want to live alone even though she found life with her sister and brother-in-law dull, and had tentatively offered Miss Hertz a job as live-in housekeeper and cook.

She had been afraid Miss Hertz would take offense at being offered such menial work by a younger woman, but instead Miss Hertz leapt at the opportunity.

"I like a clean house, a well-tended garden, and good food," she said. "It brings me satisfaction. My sister keeps her own house well, even with the laundry, and I always felt unnecessary there. Here, I can tell you will need me. And—you will let me sit with you sometimes in the evenings, to talk or to listen to the radio together?"

Pauline assured her with perfect truthfulness that she would be more than welcome, and Miss Hertz nodded, her strong features creasing into a wide smile.

"Then I will be very happy. I will have good work to do, and I will not be lonely. What more can a woman ask?"

Pauline couldn't have put it better herself.

Now here they were, ready to move in. Pauline looked down at the key in her hand, marveling. Before she could get too lost in amazement, Sarah nudged her.

"Shall we go in, or do you want to stand out here all day?"

Her tone was teasing but affectionate. Pauline smiled at her, appreciating again what a good friend she was.

"Let's go in," she said.

They walked down the path to the front door, sensing this was one occasion at least where entering by way of the kitchen would be entirely out of place. Pauline inserted the key into the lock, turned it, gripped the doorknob, and opened the door.

Inside, the front hall sparkled, a testimony to the hard work of the three women who had cleaned it. Pauline wandered through the rooms in something of a daze, unable to believe all this was hers now.

The living room with the fireplace, the owl andirons left behind by Mr. Crane at Pauline's request... the perfect place for the three of them to sit in the evenings discussing events large and small, or to enjoy each other's company in silence as they all dreamed their own dreams. The dining room with its old-gold walls... perhaps one day to see friends and family sharing meals around the table, something Pauline never thought she would be able to achieve, or indeed even wish for. The cozy green kitchen... soon to be Miss Hertz's domain, though Pauline anticipated they all would spend a great deal of their time at the table in there. Upstairs, she marveled over the tub and toilet in her very own bathroom, and sighed in satisfaction at the blue and white walls of her bedroom, re-papered at her request by the builders while they were there.

She peeked into Sarah's bedroom, a symphony in yellow and buff, just long enough to assure herself everything was as her friend wanted it, likewise downstairs in Miss Hertz's small white bedroom, and at last allowed herself to open the door into the library.

She had insisted the books remain with the house when she bought it, and Mr. Crane, certain they would bring a mere pittance at auction, had agreed. Pauline trailed one hand along the bookcases as she made a circuit of the room. So many books! Not only for her to read, but for her to continue Miss Lewis's work of loaning out to others who might also take joy in them.

Here she would work, continuing with the Emma Daring novels, no longer her secret shame. They were what had allowed her to purchase this house... she would never hide them again, no matter how trite the writing of them seemed in comparison to the work she had once dreamed of doing. Here she would finish Miss Lewis's memoirs, even if they would never see publication, as a tribute to the woman who had done such good things in her unostentatious way with a life that would seem to small to so many people. Here Pauline would still allow herself to dream of doing greater work, even while she no longer bound her happiness to those dreams.

Sarah poked her head through the doorway. "I thought I'd find you here. We have company."

"What, already?" Pauline said, startled from her musings. "We haven't even unloaded the van yet!"

Waiting by the front fence was what looked to Pauline's bemused gaze like an entire crowd of people. There were James, Ruby, and Jeremy, dressed in working clothes. There were Mrs. MacNeill and her son Angus, likewise ready to help. There was Mrs. Hansen with a covered basket, likely holding lunch for the workers. There were the Ingersolls, their Charlie already showing signs of wanting to scuffle with Jeremy. There was Iris Ferris, Ruby's sister-in-law from her first marriage. There was Arabella Warren, accompanied by her ward Jonathan, friends who Pauline had helped bring together just this past spring. Young Officer's Wallace's red head shone in the back of the crowd, and Pauline and Sarah's former landlady Mrs. Harper held a basket the twin of Mrs. Hansen's.

Pauline rested her hand on her heart as she fell back a step, stunned.

"You ladies didn't think we'd let you move in by yourself, did you?" James asked with an easy grin.

Pauline had to blink back sudden tears. It seemed she had become part of this community without even realizing it.

"Welcome," she said, after clearing her throat. "Welcome, all of you."

She had indeed come *home*.

<u>*The End*</u>

About the Author:

Louise Bates is the alter ego of fantasy/sci-fi author E.L. Bates. She lives on the New England coast with her husband and children, and when she is not writing can usually be found reading, knitting, or exploring the nearby woods and shoreline.

Acknowledgements:

It is difficult to believe we are at the end of the Pauline Gray stories—at least for now. It has been a privilege and a delight to write these stories in an attempt to capture some of the warmth and community of my hometown. I am as always thankful for A.M. Offenwanger's expert eye when it comes to editing and proofreading. Any errors that remain are my own, not hers! Thanks are also due to Kevin Bates, who has generously shared his knowledge of St. Lawrence County as well as his own memories and stories from his family. No real person has made it into this book, but those stories were invaluable in painting a picture of "life back then." Thank you to my husband Carl, who not only supports me and keeps me supplied with tea while I write, but who also drove me down many back roads as I tried to find the perfect setting for Miss Lewis's house on one of my research trips to the area. Thank you to all my readers for encouraging me throughout this journey, and for enjoying reading Pauline's adventures as much as I have enjoyed writing them.

www.ingramcontent.com/pod-product-compliance
Lightning Source LLC
Chambersburg PA
CBHW030534130626
46552CB00006B/2254